OUTCAST

# STUART THOROGOOD

# OUTCAST

## THE GAY MEN'S PRESS

First published 1999 by The Gay Men's Press
GMP Publishers Ltd, in association with Prowler Press Ltd
3 Broadbent Close, London N6 5GG

World copyright © 1999 Stuart Thorogood

A CIP catalogue record for this book is available
from the British Library

ISBN 0 85449 282 8

Distributed in Europe by Central Books,
99 Wallis Rd, London E9 5LN

Distributed in North America by LPC/InBook,
1436 West Randolph Street, Chicago, IL 60607

Distributed in Australia by Bulldog Books,
P O Box 300, Beaconsfield, NSW 2014

Printed and bound in the EU by WSOY, Juva, Finland

This book is dedicated
to my mother, Jill
— for believing.

*Preface*

I'M MARK HOLLY and I'm gay.

God, it still sounds so weird. This time last year, I would never even have thought that sentence, let alone said it aloud.

Over the last twelve months, I've undertaken a long, often painful, soul-searching journey.

One year. Doesn't sound like much, does it? Fifty-two weeks. Three-hundred-and-sixty-four days. But to me it seemed like a decade.

Coming out. It sounds so simple, doesn't it? *Coming out.* Like going down the pub, or out for a meal. But no. The coming out I'm talking about, as you most probably know, was one of the most painful things I've ever had to do.

Now, with my homosexuality out in the open, things are easier. My life is on the track that I feel it was always meant to be, and that's good. Oh, I know things can never be the same, but the way I see it, you have to embrace change, be yourself, and if someone doesn't like it... well... tough shit.

My mum and sister are great about it now. I think my sister reckons it's pretty cool to have a gay brother! Of course, to begin with, they were a bit shaken, but who can blame them? It was my dad and my brother who took it the worst, but they seem to be dealing with it now. At least in the best way they can, which I guess is as much as I can hope for. But nobody said it was going to be easy, did they?

The year I came out started off well enough. Things seemed to be going well for the band I played in. Family life was okay. But then...

Ah, well, you can find out about that later. The main thing I wanted to say here was that I hope my story will help anyone who happens to be in the situation I found myself in last year. The decision to come out is never easy, but at the end of the day it had to be mine and nobody else's – not my friends', my family's or my boyfriend's. And I hope the words in these pages will help anyone in a similar situation to make that choice for themselves, too.

Enjoy.

*Part One*

# 1

"IT'S STILL TOO slow," said Chris. He turned and glared at me as I sat behind my drum kit, sticks in hand. "Catch up, Mark. This is supposed to be a fast song, get it? Fast? As in, not slow?" The fat vocalist of Lyar grinned at his own feeble joke, cheeks reddening.

"Eat shit, Chris," I told the burly singer.

Chris turned back to his microphone without responding. "All right, lads," he said, "let's do it again. From the top this time."

I clacked my drum sticks together.

"One-two-three-four!"

Jason, the guitar player, struck the opening chords of *Stupid Smile* and we ran through the song once, flawlessly. It was easily our best, and Chris had made sure it was the first track to go on our demo CD, the one we'd recorded last week and were about to distribute to as many record companies as our meagre budget would allow.

I'd been playing with Lyar for just over a year. The band itself had been formed over two years ago, but the original drummer had moved to Turkey after the first year. Chris, the lead singer, had advertised in *Melody Maker* for a replacement. Over three hundred potential drummers had applied, including me. I was given the job without even having to audition, which, I supposed, was due to the fact that I lived near Chris's flat. Chris's flat was where we rehearsed. It's a dump, but what are you gonna do?

All of us, except Chris, were on the dole. I used to have a job, working in a chip shop, but it was hardly what I wanted to do for a living. I got booted out after I'd been there for just under a month. The reason? Well, I sort of had a problem with punctuality. But that was all in the past. Now that I had Lyar, I didn't need anything else.

We were good. Not quite as good as the Verve, but pretty close. Our music had a distinct indie sound, but Jim, on keyboards, had sneaked in a slight dancey, trip-hop kind of vibe. It was cool stuff, and I had no doubts that one day – one day soon – Lyar were going to be big. It was just a matter of time.

"All right, lads," said Chris, adjusting his microphone, "we'll do one more and then call it a day. *Tribal Sex*, yeah?"

Once again I clacked my drum sticks together for the song's intro.

"One-two-and-a-one-two-three-four!"

We launched into *Tribal Sex*, which I'd co-written with Chris last month. It was one of my favourites, due not least to its up-tempo Latin feel.

"Fuckin' brilliant," said Chris as we finished. I had to agree. Our feel was getting better and better every day. I climbed out from behind the drum kit and we all shook hands and patted backs.

There were four of us to the group. Chris, on vocals, was twenty-four. Keyboardist Jim was twenty-one. Our guitarist, Jason, was the baby of the group at nineteen. Me, I was twenty.

"Coming down the pub, Mark?" asked Jason, as I shrugged on my leather jacket, ready to go.

I shook my head. "No. I said I'd be home for dinner tonight. Mum's doing a roast."

"A roast, eh?" said Jim, folding up the legs of his keyboard and leaning it against the wall. "Any room at the table for me?" He laughed and ran a hand through his shoulder-length blond hair.

"Sorry, mate. Full house tonight. My brother, his wife and my sister and her old man. Family only, you know."

"Ah, well, think of me, won't you," Jim went on, "when I'm sitting in front of the telly with my pint and my cold kebab."

I had to laugh. "I will."

"How about you, Chris?" Jason asked the singer. "Coming down the pub? Few bevvy's?"

"No can do, mate," Chris replied tiredly. "Gotta work. Midnight shift."

"On me tod then, am I?" said Jason, pretending to be upset. "As usual."

"Maybe I'll see you down the Lion and Eagle later on," I said. "If I can drag myself away." I headed to the door. "See you later, lads. Tomorrow morning, usual time."

"Yeah, see you, mate," said Jason. I left the flat, hurried down the flight of steps and out into the cold January day.

When I got home Mum was sitting at the dining-room table, head in her hands. Dad was beside her with an arm around her shoulders. "What's up?" I asked, walking into the room. Ours was a small, terraced house with a combination lounge/dining room. It was very old. Generations of Holly's had lived in it.

Sometimes I loved the pokey little rooms and the rickety old staircase. Other times I hated them. During these times I longed for a big modern house.

One day, Mark, I promised myself. When Lyar get really big.

"Your mother burnt the roast, son," my dad told me. He was a plumber. His father had been a plumber. His father's father had been a plumber. Plumbing sort of ran in the bloodline. Not mine, though. I couldn't think of anything worse than spending my life fixing other people's waterworks.

It seemed that the plumbing tradition had come up against a brick wall in this particular branch of the family tree, though, because neither I nor my brother Nick (who worked as a lifeguard at the local leisure center) was even remotely interested in pursuing that particular dream.

"It doesn't matter, Mum," I said, putting a comforting hand on her narrow shoulder. "It's just a roast. It really isn't a big deal."

"That's what I've been *telling* her," said Dad. "It doesn't matter, Maeve. Forget it."

"But Nick and Saffron were coming round!" my mother said, suddenly coming to life. Her eyes were red. She'd actually been crying over something as stupid as a ruined joint of beef. "And Amy and Tim! They're all expecting a big dinner. I promised them a big dinner. Now what am I going to do?"

"They'll understand, Mum," I said gently. "It's not the end of the world."

Unfortunately my mother was the sort of woman who got upset about everything. The tiniest little thing could reduce her to tears. She was a very quiet, frail woman. Fifty last birthday, but looked more like sixty. My dad was fifty-four but looked at least ten years younger than that. He was a short, well-built man, Brylcreemed hair and tattoos on his forearms. You know the type. He and Mum made an odd couple, but there was no doubt that they loved each other. They'd been together for twenty-six years and had three children to prove it.

First there had come Amy, my sister. She was twenty-five and worked as a secretary. Then there was Nick, who was twenty-two, just two years older than me. I was the baby of the family. Sometimes this had its advantages. Sometimes not.

"Listen, Maeve," my father was saying, "why don't we go out for the evening? Push the boat out a bit? What about that?"

Before she could respond, my brother came home. He was a pretty muscular lad, taller than anyone else in the family. Academically, he wasn't much cop, like the rest of us, but athletically he was the best there was. After leaving school with a Sports Studies O-level, he'd scored the job at the local leisure center as a lifeguard. Nick could swim. He could *really* swim. His bedroom, before he got married and moved out, had been filled with all manner of trophies and certificates to prove his swimming excellence. Personally, I'd had to struggle to get my hundred metres when I was ten, but then, Nick couldn't play the drums to save his life, so things were pretty even between us.

Nick and I had always got on, mainly because we were so close in age. Of course, we had our arguments – what brothers don't? – but since Nick moved out we'd been getting on better than ever.

"All right, everyone?" he asked good-naturedly, dropping his bag to the floor. He was wearing Adidas tracksuit bottoms and a blue T-shirt that bore the logo of the leisure centre where he worked. He'd been married for six months, to the beautiful Saffron Cox who was a year older than him. Saffron's family were rich and for a wedding present they'd brought the happy couple a posh flat on the other side of town. But Nick always popped round to ours after work, for a cup of tea and a chat. Saffron worked as a journalist at some fashion magazine. I can't remember which one.

"All right, son," said Dad. "How's your day been?"

"Pretty good. Just popped round to tell you Saf won't be

able to make it for tea tonight. She's got to cover some launch or something." He shrugged. "Don't know much about it."

"Watch out, Nick," I said, grinning, "you sure she's not doing the dirty on you?"

"Shut it, you," he said, swatting me playfully round the head.

"Oh, that's a shame," Dad said. "We were going to go out tonight."

"Go out?" said Nick. "I thought Mum was doing a roast."

Dad ran a finger across his throat. Nick instantly got the message and nodded.

"I don't feel like going out, anyway," said Mum, looking up. She sniffed pathetically. "If Saffron's not coming, we might as well put it off for another day. I wanted it to be a proper family thing. We'll just have fish and chips or something instead."

"Suits me," said Nick. "I'm going to have a quick shower. See you all later." He turned and hurried upstairs.

"Yeah, I think I'll go upstairs an' all," I said. I left the room and went up after my brother.

My bedroom was small but cosy. The walls were covered with posters of my musical idols. There was actually a pretty big contrast, from classics like Hendrix, the Beatles and Bowie to new stuff like Republica, Garbage, Sneaker Pimps and Tori Amos. I had a massive CD collection, but my stereo was nothing special.

I slid a Portishead disc into the player and flopped down onto my bed, just to chill out. Ten minutes later, my brother came in, fresh from the shower, towel wrapped around his waist, cropped brown hair combed forward across his head.

"All right, mate," he said brightly. "Fancy coming down the pub for a drink?"

I sat up and shrugged. "Yeah, don't see why not."

"Good. But you might want to have a shave first."

I ran my hand across my chin, feeling the prickles of two days worth of stubble. "It's designer," I said.

Nick grinned. "It's a mess, you mean. You're never gonna get a girlfriend you go around like that."

"Some girls like stubble," I replied. "And anyway, maybe I don't want a girlfriend."

Nick snorted. "Yeah, right. You're a bloke, aren't you?"

I shrugged. "Where d'you fancy going?"

"Lion and Eagle? Might as well."

"Suits me. Let me just get changed – "

" – and shaved," Nick said. "I'll meet you downstairs in ten minutes."


## 2


THE LION AND EAGLE was our local. Usual pub, always busy, always jolly. The landlord, Bert, had known our dad for years. As usual, he was pleased to see me and Nick.

"All right, boys!" he said cheerfully. "How are you? How's the old man?"

"Same as ever," said Nick.

"Good, good. Your mum keeping well?"

"She's great, yeah."

"Good stuff," said Bert. "So, what'll it be, then, lads? Couple of pints?"

"Please."

It didn't take Bert long to sort out the order. He plonked the two glasses down in front of us. Nick held out a fiver but Bert shook his head, still grinning.

"On the house, mate," he said. "Call it a late wedding present, if you like."

"Cheers," said Nick and we both picked up our pints, taking deep gulps, leaning against the bar.

"So," Nick began, "how's the band? Been signed up yet?"

"Not yet. But we can't be far off. We're just about to send all our demo discs off. Someone's bound to be interested."

"Any gigs lined up?"

"No."

An odd, interested expression crossed my brother's face. "Hmm," he said.

"What?"

"Well – no promises, or nothing, right – but I might have a mate who could help you out there. He knows the manager of Forbidden. You know that new club down the road? Maybe he'll be able to get you an audition. *Maybe*."

I couldn't believe it. "A gig?" I said. "At Forbidden? For us?"

Nick nodded and sipped his lager. "Maybe. I can't make any promises, though. Better not mention it to anyone. Not just yet."

"Yeah," I agreed. "Better not get the guys' hopes up, eh?"

"Exactly."

"And what about you and Saffron?" I asked, changing the subject. "Married life still agreeing with you?"

"Brilliant, mate. It's the best thing that – " And here he paused, looking past me, an inane grin on his face.

"What?" I asked. I turned my head to follow the direction of his gaze and saw, at a table on the other side of the pub, two girls, giggling and waving at Nick.

"Not bad, eh?" Nick whispered to me. "No, not bad at all."

"What?" I hissed back, draining the last of my pint. "You're joking. You can't be serious about pulling a bird. You're... married."

Nick looked pretty incredulous when confronted with this little fact. "So?" he asked with a devilish wink. "You don't think Saf's eyeing up those male models at all these fashion doo-dah's she's always at?"

"Well... maybe," I said, "but – "

"Yeah, you're right," Nick sighed, interrupting. He looked down absently into his near-empty glass. "Most of those blokes are poofs anyway, aren't they? Model types and all that."

"Not all of them," I said quietly.

Just then Bert appeared at the bar. "You want another two, lads?" he asked.

"Yeah," I told him. "Cheers." And to Nick I said, "I'll get these."

"Oh, cheers, Mark. Then what say we head over there, eh? Get us each a bit. What do you think?"

Bert placed two more pints on the bar and I paid him. I couldn't believe what my brother was suggesting.

"Well?" Nick said as the landlord handed back my change. He seemed pretty desperate. So much so that I wondered if he and Saffron were having regular sex. "Come on. You must be gagging for it, mate. When was the last time you've had a bird?" In a lower voice, he added, "If you ever have."

"What's that meant to mean?" I snapped back. I wasn't a virgin. I'd lost my cherry when I was fifteen, to a girl in my class. Five years ago. It seemed like a lifetime back and I'd never found the experience particularly fantastic. Over-rated, if you ask me, but I'd only done it three times in all. Maybe it got better with age.

I sighed and downed half my pint in one. "Come on then," I said. "Let's go over." Perhaps it was the alcohol talking, I couldn't be sure. But what the hell?

We approached the two girls and they giggled stupidly. I couldn't help but roll my eyes.

"All right, ladies!" said Nick, pulling a chair over and sitting down.

"Hi," said the girl next to Nick. She was clearly interested in him, I could see it in her eyes.

"Fancy a drink?" said Nick.

The girl giggled again. "We'll have two vodka and orange's, please," she said, smiling sweetly. She had short blonde hair and was wearing a bright red mini-dress. Her choice of clothes was a bit over the top for the Lion and Eagle, but I figured she was probably going onto a club later.

"Vodka and orange it is," said Nick. "Hey, Mark, be a mate and get the drinks in, will you?"

The second girl stood up. She was beautiful, with red hair tied back in a ponytail. She was dressed in skin-tight PVC trousers and a white crop top. *Definitely* too up-market for the pub.

She smiled at me. "Why don't I give you a hand?"

I shrugged. "Fine by me, yeah."

We headed over to the bar. "My name's Grace, by the way," the girl said. She held out a slim hand and I shook it.

"I'm Mark."

Grace smiled. "I've always liked that name. Mark. *Very* sexy."

I could feel my face turn bright red.

Bert spotted us and approached. "Yes, mate," he said. "What can I get you? Again." He grinned.

"A couple of vodka and orange's, please, Bert."

He tipped me a knowing wink. "Right you are." He prepared the drinks and put them on a tray along with four packets of smoky bacon crisps. "On the house, those are," he said.

I laughed slightly. "Cheers, Bert."

After I'd paid, Grace and I headed back to the table where Nick and the other girl seemed to be getting on like a house on fire, laughing together. I wondered where all this was leading. Was Nick happy with Saffron? This blatant flirting of his didn't seem to be a healthy indication that he was.

I handed the drinks round and sat down beside Grace. To my embarrassment, she put a hand on my thigh. I shifted uncomfortably.

"We were going on to a club later," said the girl beside Nick whose name I did not yet know. "Why don't you two come along?"

"Love to," said Nick instantly, face lighting up with all kinds of possibilities. He sipped his lager.

I, however, was uncertain of this invitation.

Grace squeezed my thigh gently. "What do you say, Mark?" she asked seductively. "Fancy a bit of clubbing?"

I shook my head. "I don't think so."

"Neither do I, really," said Grace. To Nick and her friend she said, "Why don't you two just go? I'm sure Mark and I can find plenty of things to keep us... occupied." She smiled wickedly.

Suddenly I felt as if I were trapped in the web of the deadly Black Widow. She who mates... before she kills. But there was something oddly alluring about Grace; something enticing that I couldn't quite seem to resist.

"You sure?" said Nick. "You don't mind if Anita and I go?"

"Of course not," Grace said with a smile.

Nick turned to me. "What are you going to do?"

I shrugged. "Probably just hang around here for a bit longer."

"You never know," Grace added, smirking, "we might join you later. But then again... we might not."

Her words were making me more uncomfortable by the

second. What did she have in mind here?

Nick shrugged and got to his feet. "Well, we'll be off then. See you later, mate," he said to me. He winked, just as Bert had done at the bar.

I sat there, pint of lager in my hand, watching as Nick and Anita left the pub, laughing together.

Once they'd gone, Grace turned to me. There was a mischievous glint in her pretty eyes. "You sure you don't want to go with them?" she asked.

I shook my head. "I don't feel like it."

She downed her vodka and orange. "Do you feel like coming back to my place?" she purred, and before I could react she planted a kiss on my cheek. "Anita won't be there. So there'll be nothing to disturb us, will there?"

"You two live together?" I asked.

Grace nodded. "We're sisters."

"Sisters?"

"That's right."

"Oh." I gulped down more lager.

"So, do you want to? Come back to my place, I mean? We could go right now, if you like. I'll shout for the cab."

Again, I shrugged. "Yeah, okay. Might as well."

I didn't really want to go back to Grace's flat. In fact, the whole scenario made me feel quite nervous. But I felt weirdly obliged to go. Maybe it was because Nick had ribbed me earlier, about being a virgin, which, as I explained earlier, I wasn't.

"Excellent," said Grace, getting to her feet. "Come on then. Drink up."

I did as I was told, downing the rest of the lager and standing up. I felt a bit wobbly, because of the alcohol, but figured it was for the best. Whatever was about to unfold here would probably be easier to handle if I wasn't one hundred percent sober.

We left the pub, hailed a taxi and climbed in to the back seat. Grace told the driver her address and the car oozed away from the kerb.

"So what do you do, Mark?" she asked.

"I'm in a band," I told her. "The drummer."

"A band, eh? What are you called? I might have heard of you."

"We're called Lyar. The group's been around for a couple of years but I only joined last year. We've only just started getting serious, though. Making demos and all that."

Grace smiled. "You'll have to let me know where you're playing. I'd love to come and see you. I think musicians are so sexy." She grinned and squeezed my thigh.

It didn't take long for us to arrive at Grace's flat. It was above a pet shop and the stairway that led up to it smelt of hamster food and parrot droppings. "You'll have to excuse the smell," Grace said as she turned the lock in the door.

I followed her inside. Despite its location, the flat was pretty cool. There was a long living room with an archway through to the kitchen at one end. Two open doors went into separate bedrooms, one for Anita, one for Grace.

"Take your jacket off," Grace said, and I obeyed, handing it to her. She took it and slung it casually across a nearby armchair.

"Nice place," I told her.

She smiled and went into the kitchen. "Cheers. We only rent it, though."

"What do you do?" I called out, sitting on the armchair.

"I'm a secretary and Anita is a model."

"A model? What kind?"

"Oh, just catalogues and stuff. Nothing too glamorous." Grace emerged from the kitchen. In her hand she held two objects. A joint and a lighter. She lit the joint and took a puff before offering it to me. I'd smoked marijuana on a few occasions and had always enjoyed it. I accepted, taking a long drag. It was good stuff – potent and sweet.

"Mm, that's good," I said, handing it back to Grace. She smiled, pleased by the compliment, and took a second drag before letting me have another pull on it.

This went on until the entire joint had been smoked. Needless to say, after half a joint and three pints of lager I wasn't feeling that inhibited, so when Grace asked me if I wanted to go into the bedroom, of course I said yes.

The bedroom was a neat and tidy affair with a double bed covered with a dark blue quilt. There was a stereo on the bedside cabinet and a few CDs lying on top of it. Most of the CDs,

I noticed, were classical.

Grace closed the door and then turned me to face her. We were standing very close to one another, so close that I could feel her breath against my skin.

She smiled and then we kissed, deeply, passionately. I was wearing a simple green shirt and while we kissed she unbuttoned it, letting it fall away. I knew I was being seduced and a strange feeling began to take over – half excitement, half fear. Strangely, it seemed as though I were exploring uncharted territory, which was ridiculous since I'd had sex before on a few occasions.

My shirt fell to the floor and Grace ran her slim hands over my bare chest. I was actually in pretty good shape – not what you might call a muscle man, but I wasn't fat and I wasn't skinny. I was just an average bloke.

But Grace didn't seem to be an average woman and suddenly, her hands were everywhere. She unbuttoned my jeans and they dropped to the floor. Then she delved into my boxer shorts, feeling me.

Five minutes later, we were having full sex.

### 3

WHEN I AWOKE my head felt like someone had ploughed a chainsaw through it. The pain was unbearable. I opened my eyes slowly. It was daylight. Turning my head slightly I saw the time on the radio clock. It had just gone eight and I had to be at Chris's for rehearsals at nine.

I sat up and a fresh spear of pain stabbed my head. Grace was beside me, lying on her back. The sheet was down to her navel, leaving her breasts exposed. Carefully, quietly, I swung my legs over the side of the bed and stood up. Looking down, I flushed with embarrassment, noticing I was still wearing a condom from last night.

I peeled away the moist rubber sheath, folded it up carefully so as not to let the contents spill and took it into the bathroom where I flushed it down the toilet. Then I hurried back into Grace's room and got dressed. I decided not to leave a note explaining my absence. I had nothing to write one with and wasn't about to go snooping around the flat to find paper and pen.

Once I was dressed, I left the flat and caught a bus from the stop at the end of the road.

It didn't take long to get to Chris's, but there wasn't much point in going home first.

"You're early," he said, opening the door. He was wearing a dressing gown and his hair was a mess.

I stepped past him into the flat. "Yeah. I didn't spend the night at home."

"Oh, aye?" he said with a grin. "What's going on?" He went into the kitchen and I followed him, leaning against the work surface. "You want a coffee?" he asked.

I nodded. "Cheers. Don't suppose you've got any pain killers?"

Chris chuckled. "Sounds like you had quite a night. Check the top cupboard."

I did, and found a half-empty box of Anadin. I popped out two pills and swallowed them quickly.

"So who was the lucky lady?" he asked, handing me a mug of coffee.

"Her name's Grace. But I'm sure it was just a one-night thing."

Chris's eye held a sceptical twinkle. "Oh yeah?"

"Yeah."

The fat singer laughed. "That's what they all say, mate."

The morning passed pretty much as usual. We rehearsed all our old stuff, along with a new song Jason had written the night before, called *Some Way Out Of Nothing*. At lunch time, we had a surprise visitor to the flat, in the form of my brother.

"What are you doing here?" I asked. The rest of the band had met him before and seemed to like him. He'd obviously come from work because he was wearing the tracksuit bottoms and the blue T-shirt from yesterday. Despite the chilly winter weather, he'd not worn a jacket.

"I've got some news for you all."

"What news?" asked Chris.

"Mark'll know."

I was confused. "What are you talking about?"

Nick grinned. "You know that bloke I was telling you about yesterday? He knows the manager of Forbidden?"

Jason stepped forward, his guitar slung over his shoulder. "The night club?" he said.

Nick nodded. "I spoke to him about you lot and he had a word with the manager. He said he can get you a gig next week. So long as he likes your audition. What do you think to *that*?" Nick's grin widened. He loved playing the hero.

"That's brilliant!" Chris exploded, cheeks reddening with joy. He vigorously pumped Nick's hand up and down. "When's the audition?"

"The details haven't been confirmed yet. Matthew – that's my mate – is gonna get in touch with you. I've given him your number, Chris. All right?"

"No problem, mate. No problem."

While the band talked excitedly about what songs to play at the audition, Nick took me aside.

"So, how'd you get on with Grace last night?" he asked, grinning. "She was very impressed with you, you know?"

"What? Have you seen her?"

"Of course. Didn't she say Anita was her sister?"

"Yes, but – " And then it dawned on me. Nick must have been with Anita in the flat's other bedroom. I blushed. "Oh," I said. "Yeah."

"She said you gave quite a good performance," Nick went on. "I'm proud of you."

He laughed, but I felt sick with embarrassment.

"So, listen," he began, "you on for tonight again?"

"What?"

"The four of us. Double dating. You, Grace, me and Anita. How about it?"

"Where?"

Nick shrugged. "Dunno yet. I told the girls we'd meet them in the pub tonight. At about seven. I said they could decide."

Great, I thought, somewhat dismally. I still felt uncomfortable about being around Grace, especially as I'd slipped out that morning without so much as a by-your-leave. But I'd have to go. In a weird way, I felt as though I had to prove something to Nick.

"Yeah, sure," I told him. "Sounds like a laugh. But... what about Saffron?"

Nick was unfazed by my mention of his wife's name. He said, "Oh, she won't mind me going out. She'll probably be working anyway. You know what she's like."

I nodded, but my brother's answer made me uneasy.

"Anyway, I'd better get back to work," he said quickly. "See you in the pub tonight then. Seven, yeah?" He turned to the rest of the band, who were all still congratulating each other. "See you, lads!" he said cheerily, and then he went out the door.

After we'd finished rehearsals for the day, I took the bus home, showered, shaved and got changed. Mum and Dad were in the living room watching telly when I left for the pub and Nick hadn't come round. I figured he'd be sprucing himself up for his second night of passion with Anita and wondered what he'd tell Saffron if she caught him.

During the short walk down to the Lion and Eagle, I kept rolling over in my head the fact that my brother was cheating on his wife. I mean, what position did it put *me* in? And what would be the right thing to do? Should I tell Saffron? Threaten Nick? Let sleeping dogs lie?

Striving for reassurance, I told myself it was nothing, just a couple of one-night stands.

I arrived at the pub at a little after seven and, as I expected, Nick was standing at the bar with Grace and Anita. They were all laughing, all had drinks in their hands. I felt slightly nervous but tried to push the feeling away. Tonight I was going to enjoy myself.

"All right?" I said casually, walking up.

"Mark!" Grace cried joyfully. She sidled up beside me and kissed my cheek.

"Hi," I said shyly.

"All right, mate," said Nick. "Let me get you a pint."

"Cheers."

Anita took Grace's hand and pulled her away in the direction of the ladies' room. "We'll let you boys chat while we freshen up," she told me and Nick, a cheeky expression on her pretty face. "Nick, you can tell Mark where we're going." The two girls giggled, as if sharing a private joke, and then left.

I looked at Nick, frowning. "What was that all about?"

Nick handed me a pint and I took it, gulping at least a quarter of it down in one go. It looked as though I'd need a drink or two tonight.

"Nothing, mate," Nick said. "The girls have just decided where we're going, that's all."

"Oh?"

"We're going to Medusa's."

"Medusa's? Isn't that a – "

"A gay club, yeah," he finished.

"But..."

"I know, I know. The idea freaked me out a bit, too. To begin with. I mean, I don't like the idea of being in a night club with a load of queers, either. But then I got thinking. If all the blokes are shirt-lifters, then they won't be after our birds, will they? It's the perfect set-up, mate! As long as you don't bend over in the toilets, that is. Know what I'm saying?" He laughed a huge, hearty laugh.

But my brother's comments made me nervous, and... well, a bit pissed off. I'd never been to a gay club before, never even met anyone who *was* gay, but I had nothing against them. I knew full well that homosexuals were just normal men who happened to find other men attractive. Hell, even *I* found some blokes attractive. Sometimes I'd even fantasised about what it would be like to sleep with another man...

But I knew *I* wasn't gay. I couldn't be.

I mean, so what if sometimes I'd fancied other boys at school? So what if once or twice I'd had to struggle to hide an erection in the changing rooms after P.E.? It meant nothing.

"Pretty good plan, though, eh?" said Nick, interrupting my train of thought.

I blinked and downed the rest of my pint.

"Yeah," I agreed. "Whatever."

A moment later, the girls returned, looking giggly and excited and raring to go.

"Ready?" Grace asked, smiling. She took my hand and for

one crazy moment I wanted to pull free from her.

Anita sidled up to Nick. She looked at me and said, "Has he told you where we're going?"

"Medusa's," I replied blankly.

Grace chuckled. "It's a gay club. Won't that be a scream? You don't mind gay clubs do you, Mark?" she asked, a bit provocatively I thought. "I've been to Medusa's a few times. It's a blast." Again, more giggles.

"I've never been to a gay club," I told her.

Nick clapped his hands abruptly. "Okay, everybody. Let's make a move. I'm in the mood for a dance." His words surprised me. Nick, dancing?

Grace and Anita giggled again and hurried outside like two silly little schoolgirls. Nick and I followed.

"Don't worry, Marky, boy!" Nick said exuberantly. "So long as you stick with Grace none of those woofters'll go near you. And if they do, they'll have me to answer to. I'm not gonna let my little brother be buggered by one of *them* perverts!"

We took a taxi to Medusa's, which was a couple of miles away. We talked about trivial things, like Nick's work, the band, Anita's job. Nothing seemed to hold any substance, though. I felt strangely trapped, like a butterfly in a glass jar. I had an odd sense of wanting to be free, that I was somehow being restrained, out of reach from my real personality.

As we all climbed out of the taxi, I felt suddenly light-headed.

"You all right, mate?" Nick asked. Surprisingly, he seemed concerned. "If you don't really want to go in, we won't."

I shook my head. "No. I'm fine. I think I just need a drink."

Nick actually laughed. "That's my boy," he said. We all walked to the entrance. I'd never been to that part of town before, but I'd heard of most of the pubs and clubs in the area. I knew about Medusa's all right, but I'd never seen it. And I was actually surprised. It was just a normal club, exactly like Flamingos or Stringfellow's. Two bouncers stood at the door, normal blokes, wearing white shirts and black ties underneath dark blue bomber jackets. There was a bit of a queue as they let the punters in bit by bit, so we all got to the back of it.

The punters, there was another surprise. I don't know what I'd been expecting, never having seen a gay bloke before apart from on the telly, but they're mostly always stereotypes, aren't they? No, these people waiting to go in to Medusa's were just like Nick and I, some even had girlfriends. Must have been a pretty hot place, I thought.

Honestly, though, I'd never have said any of them were gay, and for some reason this made me feel a bit better.

The bouncers let the two lads in front of us go in and then it was us. It sounds stupid, but as they lifted the velvet rope part of me thought they wouldn't let us in because we had girls with us. But of course they did and I have to admit I blushed, feeling like a fool. Grace took my hand and squeezed it as we walked into the darkness of the night club. House music pounded at an almost violent volume and I tried to relax. "Nervous?" Grace said with a little, naughty giggle.

I grinned. "Hardly," I told her, but it was a lie. We went to the bar and Nick ordered two pints for me and him and a couple of vodkas for the girls. We all stood, backs against the bar, sipping our drinks. Nick was obviously apprehensive and I can't say I was much better. But the girls got right into it, camping it up, dancing around.

"Let's have a dance!" cried Grace, grabbing me by the hand and making me spill some of my pint.

"Careful," Nick teasingly warned her. "That's Marky's best shirt. His only shirt, in fact."

Grace smiled, all provocative, like a cat. "I prefer him without it," she said, and once again I felt my face blaze with embarrassment, remembering last night. How far away it suddenly seemed!

I put my pint down on the bar and went off with Grace. I didn't really feel that much like dancing, but I didn't want to be on my own at the bar. What if some bloke made a pass at me? Imagine that! My skin crawled with the thought of it, but looking back I probably forced myself to feel disgusted, when in fact I was aroused.

We had a few dances, Grace and I, while Nick and Anita stood at the bar. Nick seemed a little pissed off and I couldn't help but wonder if he was regretting the whole idea of this double date. I mean, he was married. Maybe his feelings for Saffron ran a little deeper than I'd at first thought, maybe deeper than even he thought.

"It's great here, isn't it?" said Grace. She threw her head back to the rhythm and her tangle of red hair swirled about her head like a fireball. She was beautiful, and as we danced I forgot all about where we were and concentrated on just enjoying myself. Glancing around, I saw that there were actually quite a few girls around and my stereotypes of homosexuals gradually began to fade.

When Anita and Nick eventually decided to come onto the dance floor, I said to Grace, "I'm going to sit this one out. You coming?"

But she wasn't ready to quit, not yet. "Nah," she said. "I'll stick around for a bit. See you later, Mark." And off she went, spinning deeper into the crowd on the dance floor, having a whale of a time.

That was when I started to get a bit more nervous and the fact that I was in a gay club standing *on my own* did nothing to ease this feeling. I wanted to grab Grace back, stand at the bar with her, chat away about nothing, as if this way I'd send out a message. *Hey, I'm not gay, all right? I'm straight! Straight as they come! Straighter!*

It was pathetic.

But what could I do? I didn't fancy asking Nick and Anita to stop doing their thing so they could hold my hand, so I just went over to the bar where my pint had mysteriously vanished. Damn! I thought, knowing I'd have to order another one but ridiculously thinking that this was some terrible task. I caught the eye of one of the bartenders, but instantly thought, *Shit! What if he thinks I'm coming on to him?*

How dense.

"Yes, mate," said the bartender, which made me, with my paranoid thoughts, think, *Mate? What does he mean by that, eh? Trying to pull me is he?*

But perhaps that's what I wanted.

I must have looked a prize pillock, standing there, mouth open, saying nothing, and the bartender laughed. "Catching flies?" he said. "Sorry, mate, we had the exterminators in last week."

For the third time that night, my face lit up like a scarlet bulb. "Er... yes," I said stupidly.

"So what'll it be?"

"Oh... a Bud. Bud, please," I said, but I thought, *Moron!*

"Bud it is." The bartender turned, opened a fridge, plucked out a bottle, opened it and handed it to me. I was thinking, *If he says "this one's on me" run for it* , but I didn't mean it.

He said, "That'll be one-thirty, please, mate," and I fumbled in my pocket like the idiot I was, pulling out a fiver and giving it to him. He worked out the change and handed it back to me as I sipped from the cold bottle. The chilly beer made me feel better.

"First time?" the bartender asked. He was tall, built like Nick and wearing a tight black T-shirt with the *Medusa's* logo emblazoned across it in white. His eyes were very blue, his hair very black and trimmed nicely. Sideburns grew to just below his ears and in the left lobe a single gold hoop sparkled.

"Sorry?" I said, sipping more of my Bud. Prickles of cold uneasiness ran across my skin. What did he mean, first time? Did he think I was... *gay*? The word stuck in my head, repeating itself over and over.

Gay, gay, gay, gay, gay. You look gay, Mark. He thinks you're gay. You must look gay. Why would he think it otherwise?

"I'm not gay," I said quickly. But of course, that only made me look like I was. Which, of course, I was. I just didn't know it then. Didn't *want* to know it then.

The bartender laughed. He said, "I didn't say you were, mate. I just meant is it your first time in a gay club? Judging by your nervousness I'd say it was. Am I right?"

Maybe it was fate, I don't know, but it was at that moment that Grace chose to make a reappearance. I could have made love to her on the spot, I was that relieved to see her. "Hey, lover," she said playfully, and kissed my cheek.

"Hi." I kissed her back, on the lips, as if I were proving to the bartender that I was a real man. I know, I know. How dumb could I be? Well, you ain't seen nothing yet.

The bloke said, "You want to watch that one, Grace. I think he's on the turn." He laughed and walked away to serve someone else.

I was outraged! What was he implying?

Grace laughed but upon seeing my angry expression, she said, "Don't worry about Andrew, Mark. He's like that with everyone."

"Not with me, he ain't," I told her in a deep voice which I guess I wanted to sound Threatening and Masculine and 'Well 'ard'. Stupid, stupid, stupid.

"You haven't got anything against gays, have you, Mark?" said Grace, tilting her head to one side and looking at me like a little bird who could read my every thought.

I sipped from my bottle of Bud. "Of course not," I told her. "I just don't like having the piss taken out of me."

This made her throw her head back and laugh. "Oh, you're too much," she said, making me feel an even bigger pratt. "Come on. Get your dancing shoes on again. It's time to *move!*"

And off we went, back on to the dance floor where Grace shook her stuff and I moved limply from side to side, thinking about Andrew and his wisecracks.

The evening went on. It wasn't that bad at Medusa's and after a few more Buds I was dancing pretty wildly. I was still looking forward to getting out of that place, though, my bladder was on red alert. "Why don't we go now?" I said to Grace.

She just looked at me, incredulity dancing in her pretty eyes. "Go?" she said. "It's only early!"

"But I'm busting," I hissed.

"There's a perfectly good toilet in here, you know," she told me reproachfully, and when I hesitated, added, "Oh, don't be such a baby. What do you think, you're going to get held down and raped? This isn't a prison, Mark." She lifted her eyebrows to make me feel infantile. She succeeded.

I looked around for Nick, but couldn't see him anywhere. "Which way is the toilet then?" I asked glumly.

She sighed, but her dancing never slowed. "Do you want me to show you?" she asked, exasperated. So of course, that was the final straw. I felt like a toddler too scared to go to the toilet in a shopping centre.

"Never mind," I said. "I'll find it myself."

"See you in a minute, Mark," said Grace.

I walked off without answering. I looked around for the toilets, but the club was incredibly dark. I couldn't see a thing. And it was as I was looking that I felt someone pinch me on the rump. I whirled. No one there. Maybe I imagined it, I don't know. But I didn't imagine the flash of arousal that went through me. Of course, at that moment in time I would never have admitted such a thing, just convinced myself that it was my overloaded bladder playing tricks on me.

*Right.*

Toilets! I kept thinking. God, didn't they use them or something?

And then behind me, a familiar voice said, "Lost something?" I turned and saw that it was that cocky barman again, Andrew. I wondered if he was the one who'd pinched me and, looking back, I'm sure at least a tiny part of me (again I didn't admit to this at the time) hoped it was.

"Do you have any toilets in this place?" I said, a bit contemptuously.

"Over there," said Andrew, pointing to a nearby door with a neon sign reading *TOILETS* above it, which made me think, God, what is it with this evening?

"Thanks," I said, and headed into the toilets. They were empty apart from two blokes about my age who were kissing and... well, feeling each other up against one of the urinals.

"S-sorry," I said, turned and went back out into the club, back onto the dance floor.

"All right?" said Grace. She was still going at it. What was it with that girl? I thought. Did she eat Duracel for breakfast?

I forced a smile. "Fine," I lied.

"See, Mark?" she said, cocking her head, shoulders moving to the rhythm. "Wasn't so bad, after all, was it?"

"No," I told her through gritted teeth.

An hour later we arrived back at her flat. Nick and Anita had gone on to another club and wouldn't be back until around six, they said.

Grace was still bouncing with energy when we got through the front door. I was completely knackered and spent at least ten minutes relieving myself in the bathroom.

"Great night," said Grace, making some coffee. "We must go there again, eh?"

"Yeah," I told her, sighing with pleasure as my bladder emptied. At that moment I would've agreed to anything.

## 4

THE WEEK PASSED. Pretty usual week. Signed on, played in the band, went home, went to sleep, woke up and so on. I didn't see Grace for a few days, but she phoned loads. "When can we go out?" she'd ask me in a whiny voice. "What are you hiding from me?" Now that was the million dollar question. What was I hiding from her? Nothing, that's what. At least that's what I thought. Of course now I see that I wasn't just hiding stuff from her, but from everybody. Even myself. But I'll come to that later.

The thing was, though, ever since that disastrous trip to Medusa's, I couldn't get the place out of my head. Why, I can't say, because at the time I swore I'd never want to go back again, despite what I'd said in Grace's bathroom. Still, there was something pulling me back there, and I think I knew what it was but – you've guessed it – would never have admitted it.

Weirdly, I kept thinking of Andrew. How normal he'd been, just a regular bloke, a bit laddish even. I never thought of gays like that. And those other two fellas, who'd been... having a good time, shall we say, in the toilets. From the quick glimpse I saw of them they'd been normal, too, regular guys like me and Nick and the rest of my band. Okay, okay, I know there's no such thing as Normal and Regular, that's just going back to Stereotype Land, isn't it? But... oh, you know. Just the sight of those two blokes kissing...

But I wouldn't allow myself to think it turned me on. Never! I told myself. Preposterous! Me, queer? No chance! On your bike, mate!

The Friday following that fateful night at Medusa's we, that is Lyar, got the confirmation for our Forbidden audition. The manager wanted to see us play at midday next Tuesday. If we were good, he'd book us in for the following Saturday. We were all so stoked. Chris, usually the biggest tight-arse you could have the misfortune to meet, even bought a bottle of champagne to celebrate. We were on cloud nine and quickly set about rehearsing. We rehearsed deep into the evening, honing our best material and preparing a couple of new numbers. I suggested that we get some more copies of our demo CD made up to give out to a few of the punters at the club. Jason and Jim thought this was a pretty good idea, but Chris was reluctant.

"Best wait until we know we've got the gig," he said warningly. "I don't want to jinx this, lads. This could be Lyar's big chance, you know."

We knew. Of course we knew. That was one of the (many) bad things about Chris; just because he started the band and he was the singer, he thought he had complete control of it and that the rest of us knew flap all about the music business. In fact, to be honest, I probably knew, more than any of them, about the industry. Course, I'd never say that. No point in causing trouble.

On Saturday Grace came round. I was stunned. I hadn't even given her my address, but it didn't take me long to realise that Nick must have. She was pretty pissed off, actually, when I opened the door. Her face was like thunder. "Is he here?" she said quietly, but her tone was way off.

"Is who here?" I asked, all innocent as she came in. My parents were in the living room watching *Blind Date* and Cilla Black's voice drifted out of the open door. I reached over and pulled it shut.

"Nick, of course," said Grace. She looked beautiful as ever, in tight jeans and a short black top. She didn't have a coat on, which was weird since it was a pretty cold night.

"Nick?" I said. "What do you want Nick for?"

"To smash his face in," said Grace.

How matter-of-factly she said it. It was weird, surreal, the way she could speak of violence in her sweet little voice. "What?" I said, frowning. "What's happened?"

"He's married, is what's happened," she said. "That bastard brother of yours is married and he's been screwing my sister!"

"Shh," I said. "Keep your voice down, will you?" I jerked a thumb in the direction of the closed living-room door.

"Is he here?" Grace repeated.

I shook my head. "No."

"You knew, Mark." She had a horribly accusing glare in her eye which made me feel about an inch tall. "You knew all along he was married and you didn't even say anything."

"I... didn't think it was my place," I said feebly.

"That's crap," she spat. "How could you, Mark? Let Anita be led on by that two-faced.. ." She trailed off, shaking her head in disgust. Then she looked up, the accusing look brighter, fiercer. "You're not married, too, are you?" She really seemed fearful that I might say yes.

"Of course not," I told her. "Listen, you're right. Nick was a bastard. But... you can't really blame me, can you?"

"Can't I?"

"No."

"You could've told me."

"I'm sorry."

There was an uneasy silence.

At last Grace said, "Well. That's all right then." She smiled and kissed my cheek. "It's not really your fault, Mark. But it makes me so *angry*. You should see Anita! She's sobbing her bloody heart out. She really liked him, you know."

All I could do was nod sadly. I felt so angry with myself! I could've stopped all this. I said, "How did you find out?"

"He told her," said Grace. "He said, 'It's been fun but time to call it a day.' Of course, Anita wasn't having that so he just told her the truth, that he was married. Just blurted it out. Bastard."

"Bastard," I agreed. "So now what?"

Grace shrugged. All the anger was oozing out of her. Now she just seemed exhausted. "I don't know," she said. "I came round here ready to flatten him. Now... I don't know. I suppose I just feel sorry for him, in a way. His poor wife!"

"Yeah," I sighed.

"She has no idea," Grace went on.

"None."

Grace's eyes lit up then. "You know what let's do?" she said, and now her voice had gone all breathy, like she had some great plan. I felt uneasy, half-knowing what was coming.

"What?" I said, dreading the answer.

"Let's teach that bastard a lesson. Let's tell his wife."

"No way," I said, shaking my head. "No way, Grace. Out of the question."

"But look what he did to Anita! It's nothing less than he deserves. Let's put his wife out of her misery."

"I said no. Grace, think what it would do to her. Nick might deserve it, but Saffron doesn't." I couldn't believe what was happening. What a mess everything was! Now I was being dragged into some plot to wreck my brother's marriage? And for what? A couple of one-night stands. Really worth it.

"You two stick together like this all the time?" Grace wanted to know. She folded her arms and looked at me impatiently. "Honestly. Men. My sister is at home, broken-hearted, because of your scum-bag brother and – "

And then Dad came through the living-room door, yawning and scratching his stomach. "Any tea in the pot?" he asked, then when he saw Grace, "'Ello, 'ello. Who's this lovely lady?" He was beaming. I was cringing.

"Hello," said Grace, smiling politely. "Mark, aren't you going to introduce me?"

"Dad this is Grace, Grace this is Dad." My voice was flat, like my mood. I wished I were a million miles away, or at the very least at the pub.

"Grace, eh?" said Dad. "How lovely." He shook Grace's hand and for a minute I thought he was going to kiss it. "Well, Mark, I'm disappointed with you," he said. "Standing here with this beautiful young woman and you don't even offer her a cuppa tea." He shook his head and tutted. "Come through, love," he said to Grace.

She smiled sweetly and I could tell she'd already won the old man's heart. She slid past me and into the living room. I had no choice but to follow.

Mum was on the armchair, feet encased in fluffy slippers, empty mug of tea in hand. Cilla Black went on and on from the telly about how sad it was that the contestant hadn't picked number three. "Maeve," Dad began, "this is Grace, *Mark's* lady-friend."

Mum's face lit up. "Hello, dear," she said to Grace, and to me, "Why, Mark, you're a dark horse, aren't you?"

I managed a grin. "Yes. Actually, me and Grace were just off out."

"Not yet," Mum said, mock-sternly. "Not till I've given this young lady a good grilling." She laughed, but I knew she wasn't kidding.

So I was forced to sit there while Mum and Dad and Grace chatted away, praying that Grace wouldn't let anything slip about Nick's fling with Anita. God, imagine that. If Saffron would've been upset about Nick's brief bout of unfaithfulness, Mum would've been suicidal. Remember how upset she was about the ruined roast?

But at last we were free to go. I hadn't been planning on going out that night, actually, but anything was better than sitting around in that house. What a relief to get outside! You have no idea.

"So where shall we go?" said Grace. Her anger at Nick had totally dissolved now; she was back to her bouncy vibrant self. But I couldn't help but wonder if she was going to go ahead with her plan about telling Saffron. I didn't want to spoil the evening, though, so I said nothing about it.

"How about... Medusa's?"

The word was out of my mouth before I could stop myself. Why? Who knows? Maybe it was fate or something. But whatever it was, the word was out there now and there was no taking it back. Grace's face lit up. "Really?" she said, thrilled with the suggestion.

I blushed, thinking, *Why did I say that? Why did I say that?*

At last I said, "Yeah. Really."

It was so weird, though. I couldn't work out why I hadn't stopped thinking about the place for the whole week, and yet now we were going I didn't want to. Except I did. But I didn't. Oh, you know what I mean.

"That does surprise me, actually, Mark," said Grace, tilting her head in that annoying way. She looked at me sideways. "I didn't really think it was your scene. Being a gay club and all that."

"Why shouldn't it be?" I said, after a pause that lasted too long. To my horror, my voice trembled slightly.

Grace shrugged. "Never mind. Come on, let's catch the

bus." She danced down the street to the bus stop and I followed. I'd cashed my giro the day before so I had a few bob. But I knew it would probably all be gone by the next day. Ah well, you got to have a good time, haven't you? Otherwise, what's the point?

And a good time was exactly what I planned to have that night, to make up for last week. I vowed not to let the fact that Medusa's was a gay club bother me. After all, I'd seen with my own eyes that gay men were just men. Nothing weird or freaky, nothing to be feared. Just normal. Like me.

The bus journey didn't take long but the whole time I just kept thinking about Anita. Nick really had been a bastard to her, but I couldn't figure out why. I'd never known him to be like that, not to anyone. Okay, he could be a bit insensitive at times, selfish, he's that type of bloke. Never cruel, though, and that's exactly how he'd treated Anita: cruelly. I knew I'd have to speak to him about it, just to keep the peace between me and Grace, really. I didn't want her to tell Saffron, I really didn't. Saffron didn't deserve that, and neither did Nick, not really. He'd been stupid, that was all, made a stupid mistake.

We had no trouble getting into Medusa's, just like before. Fortunately I was wearing smart togs, a white shirt and black trousers.

This time I wasn't nervous. Well, not much. Even then, I suppose, I was starting to get to grips with the whole gay thing, though I was a long way from coming out.

A *long* way.

Me and Grace went straight to the bar and I ordered a pint for myself, a Bacardi and coke for Grace. It wasn't Andrew who served me, but another guy, who wasn't half as good-looking.

"I just have to give Anita a call," Grace explained. "Tell her I won't be home for a bit." She smirked. "You sure you'll be all right on your own?" she asked in a baby-like voice.

I grinned. "Don't take the piss."

She shrugged, gave a funny little giggle and went off to the pay phone, wherever that was.

I leaned against the bar, sipping my pint, smiling. I felt oddly proud, like I'd achieved some major feat: standing on my own in a gay night club.

40

Grace was gone awhile, I'd finished my lager and had ordered another by the time she got back. She was wearing a worried expression. "Is everything okay?" I asked, but obviously it wasn't.

Grace said, "Anita's in a bad way."

I paused, then, "How bad?"

"She's really losing it, Mark. She was all right when she answered the phone, but then she just started sobbing. I think she might try and do something stupid."

My jaw dropped. "What... like, you mean, top herself?" I said, my voice all low and mysterious.

Grace just shrugged. "Maybe. It wouldn't be the first time she's tried. The last time was over a bloke as well."

*The last time.* So she'd tried to kill herself before. I couldn't believe what I was hearing, and all the time I just kept thinking about Nick. This is his fault, I told myself. All because he wanted to get his leg over a couple of times. Grace was right; he was a bastard.

"So what now?" I said. "Have you sent an ambulance round there or something?"

Grace shook her head. She looked really pale, as if she were about to faint. She said, "No. No, I'm gonna go back there. She needs me."

"Do you want me to go with you?" I asked.

She just looked at me, like she thought I was mad. "I don't think that would be such a hot idea," she said.

I nodded, feeling thick and stupid. "Yeah. Yeah, right." I fished into my pocket, pulled out a crumpled tenner and handed it to her. "Take this. Get a cab or something."

"Thanks," she said, accepting the money. She kissed me on the mouth. "You're really something special, you know, Mark. Hard to believe you're related to that...that scum bag."

I didn't say anything to this.

"What are you going to do?" she asked.

"Probably stay here for a bit," I told her with a shrug.

"Stay here?" She seemed surprised.

I grinned. "I'm a big boy now, Grace."

"Yeah, but – "

"But nothing," I interrupted, feeling suddenly quite brave.

"Get home to Anita. I'll be all right." I gulped down some lager, as if this would prove it.

"You're one in a million, Mark," she said, and kissed me again, on the cheek. "I'll call you." And then she was gone.

I was alone in a gay club. And it didn't bother me one iota.

Weird, huh? Quite a contrast from the week before, wasn't it?

I finished my lager, ordered another.

I was half way through it when I saw Andrew. He just appeared at the bar, same T-shirt, same grin. "Hello again," he said pleasantly.

I was startled that he remembered me, and a bit of the nervousness from last week came back. "Hi," I said in a small voice. I felt quite ridiculous, like a little schoolkid talking to the most popular boy in the playground.

"You with Grace?" Andrew said.

I shook my head, then nodded. "I was. She had to go. Her sister's... ill." It didn't seem right to tell the truth.

"Anita?" Andrew said. "Nothing serious, I hope."

I shrugged. "I don't think so. Have – you known Grace long?" I don't know why I said that, why I wanted to keep the conversation going. Perhaps I just thought it was the polite thing to do.

"Yeah, I've seen her a few times," he said. "We got chatting. I know most of the people who come here. And now that includes you. I'm Andrew by the way." He held a hand across the bar and I shook it.

"I'm Mark."

"Nice to meet you, Mark."

"Nice to, er, meet you." God, I thought. Can't I come to this place without looking a total fool?

Andrew said, "Are you waiting for someone else?"

The question threw me off guard. I didn't want to look like a total loser, so I said, "Yeah. Er, my mate said he'd meet me and Grace here later on. I suppose I'd better hang around and tell him she's gone." I laughed a feeble, pitiful laugh.

Andrew grinned, as if he knew I were lying. Strangely, I felt like he knew a lot of things about me, even though we'd never even met before. Well, not properly.

"Well, I can't stand here all night," he said. "Maybe I'll see you later, Mark."

I nodded, drank more lager, as if hiding behind it. "Yeah," I told him. "Maybe."

An hour went by. I stayed at the bar, keeping myself to myself, drinking lager. I didn't dare make eye contact with anyone, just in case... you know. But I didn't want to go home, for a couple of reasons, the first being that I knew Mum and Dad would only start grilling me about Grace and why I'd never mentioned her. Besides, Nick might be there, and I had no immediate desire to see him. Another reason for not leaving was because I didn't want to be seen coming out of a gay night club without a woman. I was no fool. I knew what the majority of society thought of homosexuality, had heard and read all kinds of horror stories about gay blokes getting beaten up. Stupid, you may think, but I wasn't about to risk anything, not on my own, anyway.

Medusa's was pretty busy, it being Saturday night and everything, so I didn't get to speak to Andrew for a while, not until things quietened down a bit. He came over, a few empty glasses in one hand. "Your fella still not turned up yet?" he asked with a grin.

I was shocked. *My fella?*

But on seeing my startled expression, Andrew actually looked a little apologetic. "Sorry, Mark. I forgot. You're not gay, are you?" There was a knowing look in his eyes. What could he see that I couldn't?

I shook my head and lifted my pint, taking a long gulp.

"Listen," Andrew began, "I get off in an hour. D'you fancy getting something to eat? A curry or something. Or fish and chips, maybe."

If Andrew asking if my fella had turned up shocked me, this nearly sent me into a coma of astonishment. "Something to eat?" I repeated. "With you?"

He looked at me with a funny slow smile on his face. "That's the general idea," he said. "What do you reckon? Since it looks like you've been stood up. I don't know about you, but I'm starving."

Stood up? I thought. Nonetheless, I *was* hungry. "Yeah," I said. "Yeah, that'll be good." I didn't know what I was doing, but it was like something was pushing me on, making me accept. The truth was, I wanted to go out with Andrew, for a meal, and a laugh. It beat going home, anyway.

"That's great," said Andrew, looking pleased as punch. "I'll finish up here and then we can go. You want another drink? On me."

I nodded weakly, but his words filled me with something between fear and excitement. What was happening? I asked myself. A gay man asking me out and buying me a drink.

Much to my horror, the excitement started to overtake the fear.

Andrew poured me a pint and placed it on the bar. "Cheers," I said in a small voice.

He said, "See you in a little while then."

"Yeah." I watched as he went off to serve some of the other punters.

Ten minutes went by. Soon the hour would be up and I'd be going on a date with a gay man. *Sick*, I thought, and yet there was something else there, that other emotion. I didn't want to go, but I did. It sounds confusing, but that's exactly what I was: confused. It was like, if I went to get something to eat with Andrew, a small part of me would know the truth, *I'd* know the truth, and that was something I didn't think I'd be able to handle. But the truth *was* there, like treasure waiting to be uncovered. Only I didn't want to uncover it. Not yet. Perhaps not ever.

Andrew, I thought. I wondered if he fancied me, but this only made that rush of heat and adrenaline grow stronger, the way you're supposed to feel when you find a girl attractive. I'd never really felt that way about anyone, not even Grace, but I was feeling it now over... *another man.*

No! I thought. I refuse to let this happen.

So I put my drink down on the bar and left Medusa's before Andrew even had a chance to notice.

# 5

TUESDAY ARRIVED, the day of the audition at Forbidden. We were all hyped as we went down to the club in Chris's van. Nick was with us, since it was he who'd scored the audition in the first place, but he and I weren't really talking. He came round to the house on Sunday and we had a row about Anita. We didn't end up coming to blows, though, which is usually what happens when the Brothers Holly have a ruck. He said it was none of my business. I said that being involved with Grace made it my business. I didn't tell him what Grace had said, though, about her telling Saffron. I was sure that would only make matters worse than they already were. The thing was, though, Nick knew I was right. He knew it was a shitty thing to have done, and even worse was the fact that I'd said right from the beginning that he was only going to get into trouble if he went off with Anita. Maybe that was what bugged him most of all – he couldn't stand it that his little brother had been right, that *I'd* known best.

We got to Forbidden dead on time, at exactly twelve noon and set up our equipment on the small stage. It was a pretty flashy joint actually, Forbidden, much nicer than Medusa's, much more up-market.

The manager's name was Ron, a young bloke, long hair tied in a ponytail, open-necked white shirt, leather trousers. He shook hands with all of us and said Nick had told him we were good. I looked at my brother, as if to say *thanks*, but he just avoided my eyes.

"Let's see what you got then," said Ron, and we rattled off three numbers flawlessly: *Stupid Smile, Tribal Sex* and a brand new song we'd written especially for the audition, *Suicidal Pigeons*.

Truly, we were brilliant, but Ron just sat there on his director's chair, arms folded.

I thought, *He hates us.*

Nick was standing behind him, looking pretty anxious. I felt a rush of love for my brother then. He really cared about Lyar, he really wanted us to succeed.

Weird.

"Well?" said Chris, his voice as anxious as Nick looked. "What do you think?"

I couldn't bear it. The idea that Ron wouldn't like our stuff made me feel quite sick.

The manager stood. He said, "Bloomin' marvellous, lads. Brilliant."

I breathed a sigh of relief and I noticed my brother do the same. Adrenaline rushed through me. Chris shouted, "Yes!" and punched a fist into the air. Jim and Jason and me all shook hands, grinning like Cheshire cats.

Ron said, "You've got the Saturday gig. But I can't offer you anymore just yet. We'll see how you go down first."

"You mean we might get a residency?" Chris asked hopefully.

"I said we'll see. Don't bank on it just yet, though. See you on Saturday. Be here at five to set up and sound check, yeah?"

Chris beamed. "No problem. Thank you. Thank you so much. You don't know what this means to us."

Ron smiled, but only very slightly. He said, "I think I've got a good idea. See you on Saturday, lads." And he left.

Nick stepped forward. "What did I tell you, eh?" he said, just as pleased as we were. "I've got you your first official gig. Now, how about you buy a drink for your new manager?"

"Manager?" said Chris. He shook his fat head. "No deal, Nick. Thanks for getting the gig and all that, but – "

"But nothing!" snapped Nick. "Listen, you need a manager, admit it. How long have you been together? Two years. And you've never played a proper gig, not at a place like this. I come along and bang, there you go, thank you very much. You've got nothing to worry about, honest. I'll be the perfect manager."

"He's right," I said.

"He's your brother," said Chris. "Your opinion doesn't count, Mark."

"Fuck you," I said. I wanted to hit him, but with his big fists he'd knock me out cold.

He sighed. "All right, Nick. I'll think about it."

I hated the way he said that, *I'll* think about it, like it was nothing to do with the rest of us if we took on a manager. Actually, I thought having Nick as Lyar's manager was a good idea. Look at the audition he'd gotten us so quickly. It was more than Chris had achieved in two years and I was sure that was where the root of Chris's reluctance lay. Just as Nick couldn't stand it when his little brother was right, Chris couldn't stand it when someone other than himself was right.

"Look," said Jason, "the bar here doesn't open yet. What say we nip down the local for a celebration drink?"

"Before the party tonight, you mean?" said Chris.

"Party?" Jim repeated.

"Yeah! We gotta have a party. This is our first proper gig we've just set up."

"Why don't we go to a club instead?" I suggested.

But as soon as the words were out I regretted them. "Brilliant idea," Nick said. "I know the perfect place. Medusa's."

I couldn't believe it. Medusa's? Why would Nick, big, tough, macho Nick want to go back there?

"No way," said Chris. "It's a bloody bent bar."

"I went there the other week," Nick went on, "with – " and here he paused, shooting a glance in my direction – "with a bird," he finished, obviously not wanting to bring Anita up.

"That's a relief," said Chris. "There's no way I'd have a flamin' bum bandit as a manager."

Nick laughed, so did Jason and Jim. "Don't blame you," said Nick. I forced a nervous chuckle, so as not to look dodgy. Mind you, the way they were talking about gays made me feel hot and nervous. "Look," said Nick, "we'll have a few bevvys and head down there. It'll be fun."

Chris shook his head. "No ta. Not for me. I don't wanna be surrounded by a load of queers. And what if someone saw us going in there? No way. No chance."

Nick shrugged. "Yeah," he said. "Suppose it was a bit of a dumb idea."

I breathed an inward sigh of relief. But still I couldn't figure out why he'd want to go to Medusa's. Number one, he definitely hated gays, at least I'd always thought so. Number two, maybe Grace and Anita would be there. The place was obviously a regular haunt of theirs.

And obviously I didn't want to go. Because of Andrew.

How could I face him, after running out on him on Saturday. I felt ashamed of that. How cowardly, how bloody pathetic of me. The bloke was just trying to be friendly, he wasn't coming on to me or anything. And even if he was, so what? We were both adults, I'd have just told him where to go. Maybe.

In the end, we decided to spend the evening at Chris's flat. We all got very drunk and very stoned and ended up sleeping there.

From Wednesday morning to Friday morning we rehearsed constantly, making sure our sound and style were honed to perfection. Nick continued to work at the leisure center, popping round to see how we were getting on during his breaks.

Chris had relented and agreed that Nick could become Lyar's manager, on a trial basis. If the gigs continued to roll in, the arrangement would be made permanent.

On Friday afternoon, Grace rang, asked if I wanted to go to Medusa's with her that night. Course, I tried to put her off, explaining that the gig was tomorrow night and I needed to stay in and rest.

"Rubbish," she said. "If you stay in you won't rest, you'll be bouncing off the walls, worrying about the gig, about the songs, all that bollocks. Come out with me. We'll have a laugh. Besides, you need to wind down. I know how hard you've all been rehearsing."

Grace had been round a couple of times during the last few days to watch us play. She thought we were good – *really* good. It was just luck that she'd always turned up while Nick had been at work. I'd told her all about the row we had and she said he deserved more than that. But I'd managed to persuade her not to spill the beans to Saffron, thank God. Anita was getting herself together, too. She hated Nick with a vengeance, but at least she was getting over him. As for Nick, he was feeling more and more guilty about what he'd done and had even suggested going round to see Anita, to explain a bit more about it. Obviously I'd told him not to. Sometimes my brother's so damn *stupid*.

But back to Friday night. The idea of going out was appealing, but Medusa's? See Andrew again? No thanks.

"Yeah, it does sound good, Grace," I said into the phone. "But why Medusa's all the time?"

"I like it there," was all she said.

"Yeah... well, I don't."

She sighed then. "Mark, what is it with you? I thought the gay thing didn't bother you."

"It doesn't."

"Then what's the problem?"

"I just feel like a change is all."

Another sigh. "Okay, where do you want to go then?"

I tried to think. My first thought was Forbidden, but since we were playing there tomorrow night, I decided against it. Instead, I said, "How about... the Lion and Eagle?"

"What?" said Grace, incredulous. "You *must* be joking."

"What's wrong with it?"

"It's full of old farts in flat caps, that's what. It's *Saturday*, Mark. Come on, can't you think of anywhere interesting to go?"

I tried.

I failed.

When I didn't respond, Grace said, "Fine. Medusa's it is. I'll get a taxi and pick you up in twenty minutes. 'Bye."

She hung up.

# 6

MEDUSA'S AGAIN. The place was like a magnet. Half of me was pulled closer, the other half pushed further away. I didn't want to go in, but at the same time I did. I didn't want to see Andrew, but at the same time I did. I didn't want to be there with Grace, but at the same I did. Confused? You should be. I know I was.

In we went. "Lighten up," said Grace, like I'd been miserable in the taxi on the way over. I guess I had been, well, maybe that's how it looked. I wasn't, though. Just... apprehensive, I suppose. I couldn't stop thinking about Andrew. The weird thing was, I really wanted to speak to him, tell him about the band. Even then I think I felt some kind of link with him, like it was meant to be, you know, us... together. After all, we'd barely even spoken to one another, he didn't even *know* I played in a band. And yet I was looking forward to telling him. And then came the obstacle. Last week, when he'd asked me to go out for a curry with him and I'd done a runner. Stupid! Probably thought I was a first-class wanker. And could I blame him?

It surprised me to realise how much it mattered what he thought about me.

Grace was her usual self, getting right into the party atmosphere, dancing, camping it up. I was more subdued. We went to the bar, ordered our drinks from a bloke who wasn't Andrew. A mixture of disappointment and relief filled me.

"What's wrong?" said Grace.

"Nothing."

"Yeah, right," she said. "Is it about tomorrow night? You nervous still?"

I looked at her, smiled. Here was a way out, an explanation for the moody way I was behaving. "Yeah, course I am," I told her. "Our first proper gig. You'll be there, won't you?"

She kissed me. "Try and keep me away," she said. "So long as Nick keeps his distance."

"He'll have to be there," I said. "He's our manager."

"Well, as long as he doesn't talk to me, then. Or sit near me. Otherwise I won't be held responsible for my actions."

I grinned. "Fine. I'll keep him away."

"You wanna dance?" Grace said.

I kissed her. "Sure."

We went on the dance floor and had a good time for about an hour. I felt suddenly really energetic. I couldn't even remember what I'd been worried about. Not really. But maybe I didn't want to remember. Maybe I'd just pushed it right to the back of my mind where I'd never have to look at it again.

I kept dancing, moving faster, really getting hooked into the music. I wasn't usually much of a dancer, but I figured if I poured all my attention into it, I'd forget. About Andrew. About those dreaded feelings that were ever so slowly inching towards the surface.

I wouldn't allow myself to think those thoughts. Wicked, evil, sick thoughts. I wouldn't do it. I wouldn't.

"God, you're full of energy tonight, aren't you?" said Grace. I looked at her. She was beautiful in the throbbing coloured lights and flickering strobes. I smiled, pulled her against me, kissed her passionately. It was as if I were saying to myself: *See? You're normal. Gay, indeed. Silly, silly daydreams. Too much time spent at this place. Playing on your mind. Making you think things that just aren't true.*

Grace pulled away from me, grinning, breathless. "Jesus, Mark," she gasped. "You *have* cheered up, haven't you?"

I nodded, the pace of my dancing never slowing. It was like I'd taken speed or done an E.

But then Grace said, "I need a breather. Let's go get another drink."

She took my hand and pulled me to the bar. The bar where Andrew stood, serving someone. My heart thudded. *Stop this!* I commanded myself.

I could feel my face turning bright red. "Hiya," said Grace. She leaned across the bar and kissed Andrew on the cheek.

"How you keeping?" he said. "How's Anita?"

"Anita?"

"Mark told me she was ill."

Grace shot me a quick glance, turned back to Andrew and said, "Oh, yeah. She's fine now. Just a... a twenty-four hour thing."

"That's good," said Andrew. "And how are you, Mark?" he said, turning piercing eyes on me. "Where'd you get to the other night?" He was grinning and I felt my face turn an even brighter shade of red.

"The other night?" said Grace, a pretty little smirk on her pretty little mouth.

"I, er, had to rush off," I said. "You were busy so I didn't... " I trailed off. I couldn't think of a way to finish the miserable excuse for an excuse.

But Andrew did not seem particularly bothered. All he said was, "These things happen. So. What can I get you two to drink? Bud for you, Mark?"

I nodded, feeling suddenly shy and weirdly flattered that he'd remembered my choice from last time.

"Grace?" said Andrew.

"Bacardi and coke, please," she said.

Andrew fixed our drinks and when I held out a fiver he

shook his head.

"No, please," I told him.

"Forget it," he said. "I like to buy drinks for my friends." There was a moment's pause while we looked at each other. Eventually I put the money away. *Don't even think about it* , I told myself. *Don't even think it because it's not true. It's not even remotely true.*

But it *was* true and the words crept into my brain no matter how much I tried to resist them.

*I fancy him.*

The evening wore on. All my energy had been used up after that little confrontation with Andrew. Okay, it wasn't really a confrontation, but it was enough to leave me feeling rattled for the rest of the night. I wanted to go, leave, get out of Medusa's, away from Andrew, away from the horrible feelings that were now racing to escape from the place where I'd locked them away. I didn't want to feel like that – who really does? – but I knew it was only a matter of time. It was like there was this clock inside me that had started ticking, and when time was up I'd have to admit the whole thing to myself, admit that I was gay.

God, it seemed like such a nightmare.

Eventually we were able to leave Medusa's, and I thought that would be it, that I'd feel better. But I didn't. Grace asked if I'd like to go back to her flat for the night, and I nearly did. But in the end I declined.

"I'd better not," I said. "Not with the gig tomorrow and all that. I'm a bit tired."

"You sure?"

"I'm sure."

So we both got in a taxi which dropped off Grace first, then me.

Mum and Dad were both in bed when I got in. I couldn't say I was surprised since it had gone one. I flopped down in front of the telly and watched a naff black-and-white B-movie. I hoped it would take my mind off everything, but it didn't. When it had finished, I went into the kitchen and put the kettle on to make myself a cuppa.

Dad came down. He was wearing his brown dressing gown

and the little bit of hair he had left was sticking up. He looked like an old clown. "Making a cuppa?" he said. "Stick one in for me, son." I did and handed it to him. We sat round the small table. "Have a good time, mate?" he asked. "That girl of yours is a looker, ain't she?"

I grinned and nodded, sipped some tea. "Dad," I said, after a thoughtful pause, "have you ever, you know, been involved with someone and then... liked someone else?"

He looked at me for a moment, and then a wicked grin split his face. "You got your eye on another young lady?" he said.

I forced a smile. "Yeah," I lied, thinking, *Christ, if you only knew.*

Dad said, "Listen, mate, here's the advice my old man gave me. You're only young once. Sow a few wild oats. Get out there. Play the field. 'Cos as lovely as your Grace is, you don't wanna be tied down. Not yet. Not at your age."

Great help. I didn't *want* to play the field... not with another bloke. At least, that's what I tried to tell myself.

"Hey, cheer up," he said. "Don't get too bogged down in life. Remember – you're only young once, yeah?" He laughed. "I'll take this upstairs," he said, raising his mug a bit. "See you in the morning, mate."

"Yeah," I said. "See you in the morning."

I watched as he ambled away, thinking *You hardly even know me.* It was true. He didn't. But how well does anyone know anyone? When it comes down to it, how well do you even know yourself?

I woke up to the unpleasantness of Nick shaking me. "Get up, get up!" he yelled. I opened my eyes slowly.

"What?" I said. "What's the matter with you?"

"It's Saturday, ain't it?" he said.

I turned my head slightly to see the radio-alarm on my bedside. It had just gone midday. "The gig's not for ages," I said sleepily.

"We've still got to rehearse," said Nick. "Come on, get up, get dressed and be downstairs in five minutes."

"Sod off," I said.

Nick swatted me round the head. "Get up. This gig has got to be perfect. Downstairs. Five minutes."

"All right, all right," I said. Nick left my room. I thought, *God, what is it with him?*

I got out of bed, showered, shaved and dressed and went downstairs. Nick was waiting in his knackered green Nova.

"'Bout time," he said.

We drove to Chris's flat. Jim and Jason were there, everything was set up. We rehearsed and rehearsed.

At half four we bundled all our gear into Chris's van and drove to Forbidden. Grace was waiting outside, looking gorgeous in tight black trousers and this really elegant-looking dark blue jacket with flared sleeves. My first thought was *Shit!* because Nick was with us, but Grace was cool about it. She didn't scream abuse at him, as I thought she might. She just ignored him. He did the same, but I could still see the flashes of guilt in his eyes. At least he *felt* like a bastard.

"Hi," Grace said. We kissed, deeply, which made me remember the first time we'd made love, nearly a month ago now. I introduced her to Jim, Jason and Chris, who all looked jealous of me. I felt on top of the world, all thoughts of Andrew and Medusa's having been shoved firmly away. Things were going well for the band and I had a beautiful girlfriend. What else was there?

One of the bar staff let us in, a girl whose name tag read *Ethel.* "You the band?" she said.

Chris stepped forward. "Yeah."

"Go round the back," Ethel told him. "Someone'll let you in and you can set up."

"Right. Cheers."

It didn't take us long to get sorted out and sound-check and before we knew where we were, the punters started to arrive. The place looked different filled with people, the lights dimmed and to say we were nervous would have been an understatement. Chris announced, "Hi. We're Lyar. And we'll be your entertainment for the evening."

It was cruel, but I had to smile when his voice stumbled slightly.

We launched into our first song, *Stupid Smile.* The reaction was lukewarm. I began to sweat. For the second number, we played *Suicidal Pigeons*. That's where things started to look up; a few punters took to the dance floor.

By the fourth song, *See Thru*, we had the place rocking. I was really getting into the vibe, slamming my sticks against the skins. Chris's voice sounded amazing, I had to admit, and Jason and Jim were on top form. I saw the manager, Ron, standing nearby, grinning, tapping his foot.

And Grace. That's what really made it for me, that she was there; grinning, clapping, dancing, winking.

By the end of our set, the euphoria among us was amazing. The club clapped and cheered their approval and I thought, *We did it, we bloody did it!*

Once the cheering had stopped, we climbed off the stage, went straight to the bar and ordered pints all round and a glass of white wine for Grace, who couldn't stop kissing me. "You were brilliant," she gushed. "You were fucking amazing!" I was too choked up to speak. Who could have thought how wonderful playing a gig could be? Those suits could stick their executive jobs, their big business firms, being normal, running a day-to-day routine, being boring. Forget that! Rock 'n roll was all I wanted, all I would ever want.

The manager, Ron, approached us. "Lads, lads!" he beamed. "What can I say? They loved you!"

Chris grinned. "They did, didn't they?"

A couple of giggly eighteen-year-olds came up and shyly asked us all for our autographs. What a feeling! That someone wanted my signature. With a huge flourish I signed a napkin. *To Jodie, love Mark.*

They went away, giggling to each other.

"So, a residency," said Ron. "You want a regular spot?"

We all looked at each other, eyes practically out on stalks, smiles stretching out for miles. Did we want a regular spot? Was the Pope a Catholic?

But Nick said, "We'll think about it."

A heavy silence fell.

"What?" said Chris.

Grace simply glared at my brother, hate in her eyes. I thought she was going to leap at him and scratch his eyes out. In fact, I'd thought that all night and was surprised how placid she was being. Pleased, too. I didn't want tonight to be marred.

"We'll think about it, Ron. We'll let you know."

Ron shrugged. "Suit yourself, mate. But you'd better not muck around. I don't offer residencies every day." He walked off.

"Are you out of your fucking mind?" Chris fumed.

Grace mumbled, "Pretty accurate description if you ask me."

"The longer we hold out," Nick explained, "the more money he'll pay."

"The longer we hold out?" Chris said. "Nick, the money isn't important. They loved us tonight. It won't be long before we get a record deal, I know it. It doesn't matter if we play here for free. And if you're going to be our manager, you've *got* to understand that."

Chris was right. The money wasn't important. We'd been paid eighty quid for tonight, which was only twenty each, but that wasn't the main thing. Exposure was. Forbidden was a pretty classy joint too, and I knew for a fact that a lot of bands would give their right legs for the opportunity of playing there on a regular basis.

Nick just looked at all of us. He knew we were right and he also knew that if he tried to come on as the big tough manager, he'd be out the door. So he just said, "Fine. Have it your own way. But just remember who got you this gig in the first place."

I said, "You didn't get us the gig, Nick. You only got us the audition."

"And you'll get a smack in the mouth if you don't shut it," he snapped. Then to all of us, "Fine. I'll leave you losers to it." He sneered. "We'll just see how far you can get without someone like me." He turned and walked off.

"Good riddance," Grace called after him.

Chris gulped down a mouthful of lager. He said, "I gotta tell you, Mark, your brother is a first class arsehole."

And for once, I had to agree with him.

## 7

EVERYONE WAS PLEASED that Nick was out of the picture, even me. Although I was grateful he'd helped us out, it was obvious he was getting too possessive with the band already, like he wanted too much control. And I thought Chris was bad! Really, it was for the best that Nick had thrown the towel in.

At about two Grace and I left Forbidden. The other lads were more than happy to stay there drinking, but us two wanted some time alone. We went back to Grace's flat. Anita wasn't there, she was staying at a mate's, so we had the place to ourselves.

The minute we got in the door Grace started kissing me, pulling my shirt off. We were both pretty pissed and stumbled drunkenly into the bedroom. "Fuck me," she kept saying in this hot, breathy voice I'd never heard her use before. "Fuck me." And even though I was a bit plastered, her words still surprised me. It was surreal; sounded totally out of character. But I did as she asked, twice. Once in the missionary position, and then again in doggy style, which I'd never done before. But that was all we could manage before we crashed out totally.

I left early the next morning, before Grace woke up. I felt guilty for just slipping away again, but for some reason I couldn't bring myself to stay. I felt like I'd cheated on someone, like I was a fake or something, a thief even. But I couldn't, for the life of me, work out where all this had come from.

I was tired when I got in, knackered to tell the truth, and had a few hours kip.

When I woke up, at around two, the house was empty. A note on the kitchen table explained that Mum and Dad had gone round to my sister's for Sunday lunch and wouldn't be back until around seven. That suited me fine. I felt like I needed the house to myself, to get my head together, chill out a bit after the last couple of days.

After a while, I popped out, just into town to pick up a paper and a pint of milk since we were out.

That's when I bumped into Andrew.

He was walking in the opposite direction to me, paper under his arm. He was wearing the same leather jacket I'd seen him in a couple of weeks back. He recognised me straight away. "Mark!" he called out. I grinned and said hi. Despite everything, I was pleased to see him. We shook hands; his grip was very firm.

"How are you?" he asked, like I'd known him for ages. The funny thing was, I felt like I had.

"I'm fine. Bit tired. But otherwise fine."

"Everything all right after the other week?"

"What?"

"You know, that emergency, when you had to dash off? Remember?"

I actually blushed. "Oh," I said. "Yeah. It's fine."

"It was a shame that, wasn't it?"

"Yeah." I wondered where all this was leading. "You not working tonight, then?" I asked, feeling awkward, wanting to steer the conversation elsewhere.

"Not till Tuesday. I'm taking a well-earned break. Saving up for a new motor."

There was an uncomfortable silence. We both looked at each other, as if we wanted to say something but didn't dare. I was attracted to him, and I hated myself for it. Nevertheless, it was true.

But as I said earlier, I'd fancied other men before, fantasised about them, even.

It was just a phase, though. Just a phase.

A horrible voice in the back of my mind whispered, *No phase lasts for seven years, Marky. Since you've been thirteen you've liked other blokes. Don't deny it. Only idiots ignore the truth.*

"How about you come round to my place tonight?" Andrew asked, abruptly.

The question took me aback.

I said, "What?" but already my heart was beating faster, my veins were racing with adrenaline.

He put his hands out in front of him, as if surrendering. He was grinning. "It's all right, I know you're not gay," he said, and I prayed no one was around to hear. "Just as mates, I mean," he went on. "Make up for the other night."

Did it mean I was gay because I was thrilled he'd asked me? Did it mean I was gay because I started to sweat with anticipation? Please no. Surely not. It couldn't...

"All right," I said, before my thoughts got too crazed. "Just as mates."

"Yes." He nodded. "Whereabouts do you live? I could come and pick you up or – "

"No," I said quickly, a little too quickly if I'm honest. "No, er, how about we meet in the Lion and Eagle? It's a pub. You know it?" Immediately I regretted the suggestion. What if someone saw me? Meeting a gay? What would they think?

"Yeah, sure I know it," he said. "Meet you at about seven?"

Seven. Mum and Dad would be home then. "Perfect," I said, relaxing a little. I told myself that no one knew Andrew was gay; you couldn't even tell. So what was the big deal?

"Excellent," he said. "Well, I'd best be off. See you at seven, Mark."

"Yeah," I told him. "Seven. See ya."


I left a note on the table for Mum, Dad and anyone else who happened to be around later. *Gone to meet a mate. Don't know when I'll be back. Love, Mark.* I hadn't seen Nick all day. He was probably pissed at me because of what happened after last night's gig.

I set off to the Lion and Eagle at quarter to seven. It was a short walk and I noticed Andrew hadn't yet arrived. The place was pretty busy, it being Sunday evening, but most of the blokes in there were all past their sell-by date, if you get my meaning, so it wasn't too bad. Bert greeted me with his usual cheery grin. "All right, mate," he said. "Pint?"

"Please."

He got my order and I paid him. I wished Andrew would hurry up. I didn't want to stay in the pub on my own and the sooner he got there, the sooner we could leave. I was looking forward to seeing him, but I wouldn't admit the real reason why. Even though I knew, deep down.

I sipped my pint, looked around anxiously, wishing again that I hadn't suggested the pub for our meeting place. Nobody's looking at you, I tried to assure myself.

Andrew turned up ten minutes later, a little out of breath. "Sorry I'm late," he said. "Traffic."

"You've got your car?"

He nodded. "It's only a Mini."

"Better than nothing," I smiled. "Which is what I've got."

He laughed.

"You want a drink?" I said.

"Er.. .yeah, why not? One can't hurt. I'll have a lager, please."

Bert came over. "Bert, this is my mate Andrew," I told him. "Andrew, meet Bert."

"All right, mate," said Bert, predictably.

Andrew said, "Nice to meet you, Bert."

"Can I have another pint, please," I said and Bert nodded, sorted it out and I paid.

Once he was gone, Andrew said, in a sort of breathless voice, "I'm glad you came."

I just looked at him. I felt weird all of a sudden, kind of giddy and sick – but pleased all the same. "Yeah?" I said.

He nodded, took a sip from his glass. "I didn't think you would. After last time. I thought you'd go and do a Cinderella on me again."

I had to laugh. "Is that what you call it? I told you, I had an emergency. I forgot to do something. I *had* to go."

"No you didn't."

Now that threw me. It was like, suddenly, he could read my mind, he knew what I was thinking, what I was going to say. And, oddly, that was one of the things I found attractive about him. It was as if he knew me, inside out, and we'd hardly even spoken before.

We finished our drinks quickly and went outside to the black Mini. The alcohol had softened my awareness, as it tended to do. I know if I'd have been sober, I'd have been darting my eyes around everywhere, looking out for people I knew, people who might put two and two together... and maybe come up with the answer I didn't yet want to reveal to myself.

I got into the Mini, Andrew started it up and pulled away.

We spoke little during the drive to the flat, but the atmosphere wasn't uncomfortable, more peaceful.

60

Andrew's flat was in a pretty up-market part of town. It was nicer than any flat I'd been in before – Nick's, Chris's, Grace's. It seemed Andrew earned quite a bit, for a bartender. "Nice place," I said, sitting down on an armchair in the living room. An archway went into the kitchen and Andrew disappeared through it, returning a few minutes later with a couple of cold cans of Foster's. He handed one to me and I accepted gratefully.

"It's only a one-bedroom. It used to be my mum's," he said, somewhat distantly. He sat down on the sofa, opened his can but didn't drink from it. Then he said, "She signed the lease over to me when she found out I was gay."

The words fell like bombs. All I could say was, "Oh," like an idiot.

Andrew grinned and had some of his Foster's. "Touchy subject with you, isn't it?"

I couldn't think of an answer to that. I lifted my can and drank. Again it was like I used it as some kind of shield, or security blanket to hide away from reality.

Andrew shook his head, as if shaking away the subject matter. "You hungry?" he asked.

I was. "Yeah."

"Fancy some pizza? My treat."

"Mm, sounds good."

He placed his can on the small coffee table and went to the phone. A pile of leaflets were sitting next to it. "I think I've got a coupon around here somewhere, you know. Buy one, get one free." He smiled at me. "I love discounts," he said, as if confiding a special secret.

I felt good. Relaxed. I also felt stupid: stupid for worrying if someone saw me with Andrew. They could go jump as far as I was concerned. I was having a good time.

Andrew ordered the pizza. A meat feast with everything on it. He found the coupon eventually, so we got two for the price of one. While we waited for them to arrive, we chatted. Nothing heavy, just everyday stuff. I told him all about Lyar, about the gig the other night and how we'd scored the residency at Forbidden. He said he'd love to come see us play some time. I told him that'd be great, but I couldn't help thinking what

Chris and the others would say about that. It made me feel really guilty. Although I'd only known Andrew a short time, we already seemed to be the best of mates; the line had dissolved. You know, the dreaded *Gay/Straight* line.

At least, I thought it had dissolved. Until the pizza arrived.

By that time we were both on our third Foster's. Andrew paid the delivery boy and bought the two large boxes through to the living room, where we tucked in seriously.

Then Andrew said, "I'm really glad you came tonight, Mark."

I swallowed thickly, uncomfortably. "You said that already," I pointed out, which made him look away.

"Yeah. I know," he said, and all of a sudden he seemed really shy, like he was embarrassed. I started to sweat. He looked up and his eyes were different, clearer somehow. This time I had to look away; I don't know why. Maybe if I'd've kept looking, I would've seen the truth, and that thought scared me shitless. Because I didn't want the truth, even though the truth was there, waiting to be dealt with.

*I didn't want to be gay.*

"I really like you, Mark," Andrew said, and that really ruined the evening. It was just like that song: *And then I go and spoil it all by saying something stupid like I love you.*

I forced a less than normal laugh. "Shut up," I said, mockseriously. But he just looked away and chewed slowly on his pizza. I felt like I'd hurt him somehow, but that was just stupid. All he'd said was *I like you.* I liked him – as a mate. At least, that's all I wanted it to be. I had to keep fighting it, that horrible truth. It was like swimming against the tide, away from reality. You try and try and try, but you can't win, you can't *ever* win. Truth beats everything. In the end.

I said, "When did you know? That you were... "

The word stuck in my throat.

"...gay?" I finally finished.

"I always knew," he said.

*Always knew.*

"Even when you were younger? Like, thirteen, fourteen?" I wanted to stop, stop asking these questions. What if I found something out I didn't want to? But I felt this great need, a strong urge to keep going, to push on, go deeper down, further in.

Andrew nodded. He fixed his eyes on mine. Such beautiful eyes.

"Even then," he said. "But I didn't want to face up to it. Of *course* I didn't. I don't think anyone does."

Oh, how I could relate to *that!*

"I just used to tell myself it was a phase, you know, like you do, that I was curious, that I'd grow out of it. When I was sixteen, I used to get erections in class, thinking about men, you know, fantasising and stuff. I used to go home and masturbate over the thought of other lads. But even then I wouldn't admit it. I wouldn't think: I'm gay, it doesn't matter. I'd just go back to telling myself it was a phase, or that I wasn't *really* attracted to the other boys."

I sat there, nodding. My throat felt like it had closed up. Everything Andrew said touched a nerve inside me. I, too, had tossed off over boys at school. I, too, had just tried to convince myself it was a phase. Jesus, I was *still* trying to convince myself now, at the age of twenty.

I wanted to go home. I wanted to just get up and go round to Grace's and bang her brains out. Anything to make it all go away, to forget Andrew's words. But it was like I was stuck there, bound by some magic spell.

I put my half-eaten slice of pizza back in the box. My appetite had gone.

"Are you all right, Mark?" Andrew said. "You look pale."

"I'm fine," I said woodenly. I downed some beer. It didn't help. "When *did* you admit it to yourself?"

Why did I ask it? Who knows? But, for some crazy reason, I needed to find out.

"When I was about eighteen," he said. "When I lost my virginity. To a girl. I didn't feel anything. And afterwards, I just knew. It just... I don't know, clicked into place, I guess. Even though it had been there all along. That was when I really, really knew it." He shook his head sadly. "It was a terrible time for me."

I nodded. A horrible memory came to me then. When I was about seventeen. At school. One of my mates had a skin mag and we were flicking through it. On one page there was this phone-sex advert thing with pictures of two blokes kissing. The caption below read: *GAY VIRGIN TAKING HIS FIRST STIFF COCK.* Another: *GAY GUYS WITH FAT COCKS SUCKING AND FUCKING EACH OTHER.*

I remembered getting hard, aroused. And all the time telling myself, *It's not really the blokes you're getting off on. It's the topless bird on the page opposite.*

Three years later, sitting there, in Andrew's flat, those memories swirling in my head, his words ringing in my ears, I thought I was going to throw up.

And for the very first time the forbidden sentence rose up in my head.

I. Am. Gay.

"Mark?" Andrew said. "You sure you're okay?"

I nodded.

"I've got some aspirin if you want it."

"I'm fine," I said. I picked up my can of Foster's and finished it off. "I'd better be going, actually."

Andrew looked a little disappointed. "Already? You've hardly touched your pizza."

"No, really. I... have to go now."

"At least stay for another beer."

"No – "

"Go on. If you get too tired you can crash out here."

Now that thought really scared me. Because if I stayed the night I might want to... we might end up...

"One more beer," I said. "Then I'll have to go."

Andrew grinned. "Excellent." He got to his feet, went to the kitchen and brought back a couple more Foster's.

As we drank, he said, "That night, in Medusa's, when I first saw you. You said you weren't gay."

I looked at him, can held in front of me. "Yes," I said, very slowly.

"Was that true?"

I froze. My heart pounded in my chest. A surge of adrenaline rushed through me.

"What?" I said.

"Was it true? You're not gay?" His voice was weird, shaky, as if he were nervous of the answer.

"Of course it was true," I told him, after a pause that seemed to last forever. And then I laughed. "Of course I'm not gay." More laughter, slightly hysterical now.

Looking back, I don't think I could've made the fact that I was lying any clearer.

More Foster's went down my throat but it offered little relief.

Then Andrew said, in a strange, sympathetic tone, "Mark. There's nothing wrong with finding another bloke attractive."

"What are you talking about?" I snapped crossly. "I know there isn't. I just don't happen *to* find other blokes attractive. I told you. I'm. Not. Gay."

He shook his head. "Sorry. Jesus, I'm so sorry, Mark. I just thought – hoped... " He broke off. He looked ever so ashamed. "Never mind," he said at last.

His words made me shiver with arousal. *He fancied me.*

"Yeah, well I'm not gay." I finished the contents of my can. "I have to go now, Andrew." My voice was cold. But it had to be.

"Please don't," he said. "I'm really sorry."

"Don't worry about it. I have to go now. Gotta rehearse tomorrow."

"At least let me drive you."

"You've been drinking. No, it's all right. I'll get the bus."

"Will I see you again?" He sounded hopeful, and God knew I wanted to see him again, but I just shrugged.

"Dunno," I told him bluntly, then, "'Bye."

I left without another word.


I caught the bus at the end of the road. Luckily I had some change on me. All the way home I kept thinking about Andrew, about what we'd discussed. *Bastard, bastard, bastard!* I kept telling myself. He'd opened doors in me, doors that led to places I didn't even want to think about, let alone visit.

*Bastard!*

And then another part of me saw it all in a new light. Andrew fancied me. He'd said he hoped I was gay, just as good as, anyway.

The adrenaline rush came, the pounding heart. I wanted to

cry, something I hadn't allowed myself to do for years. I hated Andrew then. But I hated myself more.

I got off the bus at the nearest stop to my house and as I walked I pushed everything he and I had talked about far, far away. I vowed never to see him again, never to go to Medusa's, forget it all and concentrate on my relationship with Grace. It was the way it had to be, the way I wanted it to be.

I got to my house and rang the doorbell. Mum answered, wearing her best Sunday frock, the one she'd worn to my sister's. "Hello, love," she said. "Grace is here for you."

"Grace?" I was confused.

"Been here awhile. She's in the living room."

I shrugged off my jacket, slung it on the newel post and followed my mum through. Grace was there, on the settee. "Hi," she said, looking at me with serious eyes.

"What's up?"

"We need to talk."

We went upstairs and sat on my bed. "What's this about?" I asked her.

"It's Anita," Grace said. "She's pregnant."

## 8

I ASKED THE only question that counted. "Is it Nick's?"

Grace just looked at me. "Of course it is," she said. "It must be. My sister isn't a slag."

"Oh, God," I said. I put my head in my hands. Oh, I could've have done without all this. Clutching for hope, I asked, "Is she sure?"

Grace nodded solemnly. "She's done a test. She's going to the doctor first thing tomorrow morning, to confirm it." There was a long pause. Then Grace dropped the second bombshell: "Mark, she wants to keep it."

"She can't." That was my first reaction, but then Grace glared at me and I wished I hadn't said it.

"Why can't she? It's her baby, she can keep it if she wants. Just because that scumbag brother of yours knocked her up." Grace's voice was getting higher and louder with anger. I put a finger to my lips. I didn't want Mum and Dad hearing about this.

"Has she told Nick?" I asked.

Grace shook her head. "No. She wants to be sure. But he *has* to know."

I wanted to run. I just kept thinking, This isn't fair, why is it all being heaped on me? It was bad enough I was so confused about my sexuality, about Andrew and all that shit. Now I had to deal with my brother's problems, as well? It was torture. What would Mum and Dad say? Mum – who's always wanted grandchildren. But not like this.

And what about Saffron? What was she going to do? She'd flip, kick Nick out and then divorce him. His life would be ruined.

I said, stupidly, "What a mess."

Grace just sighed so I put my arms around her and we flopped back on the bed. We just laid there for ages, cuddling, not speaking.

And all the time I thought of Andrew.

Grace left about an hour later. I'd promised her that I'd tell Nick as soon as possible. We'd both decided it would be better coming from me, though I was dreading it. But I would do it, for Grace. I dialled the number of his flat. Saffron answered.

"Hello?" she said. I thought, *You poor cow.*

"Hi, Saffron. It's Mark. Is Nick there?"

"Oh, hi, Mark! Yeah, he just got out of the shower. Nick! Mark, for you!"

My brother came on a few seconds later. "All right, mate," he said.

"Nick, I need to speak to you."

"I'm listening."

"Not on the phone."

"Why not?"

"Because it's very important. I'll meet you in the pub in ten minutes."

"Piss off, Mark. I don't want to go out. I've got work in the morning."

"Nick, please. This is *very important.*"

My brother sighed and there was a long pause. At last he said, "All right, fine. But it'd better be good." He hung up.

Nick was already at the pub when I got there. He'd ordered us both a half of lager and was sitting at a table in the corner. His face was full of rage. "Well?" he barked. "If you're going to apologise about what happened yesterday you can – "

I thought, *You bastard.*

"It's Anita," I told him, cutting him off. "She's pregnant with your kid."

There. I'd said it.

Nick just looked at me, mouth open. His eyes were bulging. "What?" he said.

I repeated, "Anita's pregnant with your baby, Nick."

"Liar."

The word was like a slap in the face. It hadn't occurred to me that he might think I was lying. For a while we both sat there, not looking at each other, not speaking. We'd drunk most of our beer before he said, "What am I going to do?" He was crying. My brother, crying. I couldn't believe it, I just sat there, looking at him like an idiot.

"She's keeping it," I said. How I hated myself for it. Rubbing salt into my own brother's gaping wounds.

He stared at me with wet eyes. "She can't," he said. All the fight had gone out of his voice, all the arrogance. It was like there was nothing left of him. It pained me deeply to see my own brother, the bloke who'd been my role model all my life, even more than my own father, looking so pathetic.

"You have to tell Saffron," I said.

"No! She can't find out about this. I'll... I'll talk to Anita, make her see sense. She can't do this to me. She can't. I love Saf! I don't want to lose her."

"You should've thought of that before," I said, getting angry now. "Why weren't you more careful? Why didn't you use a condom, for Christ's sake?"

Nick didn't respond at first. He looked into his glass, as if the answer might be found floating at the bottom of it.

"I didn't think I'd be caught out," he said sadly.

I shook my head. "None of that matters now, Nick," I

told him fiercely. "We've got to work out what to do next."

"We?"

"I'll help you out as best I can."

He smiled. Despite everything, he was grateful for my help.

"First you've got to tell Saffron. You've got to."

He wept openly. "Mark... I can't do it."

"You have to."

He shook his head.

It went on like this for the best part of an hour, me telling him to do one thing, he refusing. In the end we agreed to wait to hear from Grace tomorrow, after Anita had been to the doctor's and had it all confirmed. If she was definitely pregnant, Nick would tell Saffron and brave the consequences. What happened next would all depend on Saffron's reaction.

Nick and I went our separate ways. I really felt for my brother. Imagine having to go home to his wife, knowing what he did. Talk about a fate worse than death.

When I got home it had gone eleven. Mum and Dad were up, watching some film. They asked me to join them but I was too rattled to concentrate and went straight to bed. I wondered about the consequences this whole pregnancy thing would have on our family. As I've already said, Saffron's family were rich and respected and I knew for a fact that her parents had been less than thrilled with the prospect of their daughter's marriage to my brother. What would they say about this? And, oh, my poor mum! She'd be utterly devastated by the shame of it all.

As I laid there, in my dark bedroom, I thought of Andrew. I wanted to tell him about it, ask his advice. It was mad! I hardly knew the bloody bloke, and here I was, wanting to tell him about my family problems.

What was it all about, eh? Tell me that. What was it all about?

The next morning I woke up, dreading the day ahead. I went round Chris's flat first thing and we all rehearsed, ready for our second gig at Forbidden on Saturday. Twice I mucked up, missing several beats on a couple of songs.

"What's with you, Mark?" Jim asked

"Hangover," said Jason, with a grin.

I wished they'd all piss off.

I couldn't stop thinking about Nick.

And then, for a minute, I forgot about Nick and thought of Anita. Poor Anita. Why feel sorry for Nick? It was his fault Anita was pregnant, and now she had to live with that, she had to live with that baby, all because my brother was too dense to use protection.

More than once during that day's rehearsal I almost threw my sticks down and went home to find out what was going on. But I didn't. What would that solve? At least I had the band to concentrate on, the word *concentrate* being used in the loosest possible sense, of course.

We called it a day at about six. Jason, Jim and Chris all went down the pub, but I went straight home.

"What's the emergency?" said Chris.

I shrugged. "No emergency. I just have to get home."

"Grace waiting for you, is she?" said Jim. He smiled and winked. All Jim thinks about is sex.

Sex, however, had caused enough damage as far as I was concerned.

I took the bus home, no big surprise there. I didn't ring the door bell because I had my key, but even as I turned it in the lock I knew with a horrible certainty that the worst had happened.

And my suspicions were proved correct when I went into the living room.

Nick was standing, looking guilty. Mum was on the settee, Dad beside her. Mum was crying, Dad had his arm around her trembling shoulders. It had started. The destruction of the Holly family.

"What's going on?" I asked stupidly.

Nick looked at me. "What do you think?" he said.

Then Dad looked at me. "You knew?" he said.

I had to nod. Dad said nothing, he just kept comforting Mum who kept sobbing and wiping her eyes on her apron. I turned to Nick. "Have you told Saffron?"

He nodded sadly. My heart ached for him.

"What did she say?"

Nick pointed to the floor. There were two sports bags there, bulging. I guessed his stuff must have been in them. "She kicked you out?"

He nodded.

"I don't fucking blame her," said Dad. This shocked me. My old man was no angel; he swore all the time. But never the eff word.

My mother looked up. Tears glistened in her eyes. "How could you, Nick? How could you do that to Saffron?"

"I don't need this," Nick said, shaking his head. He picked up his bags and left the room, then the house. The front door slammed, sounding like a bolt of thunder.

"I'll go after him," I said.

I didn't have to go far. He was sitting in his Nova on the edge of the kerb, sobbing his bloody heart out. I knocked on the window and he looked up, red-eyed. Christ, and I thought *I* had some problems. He unlocked the door and I got into the passenger seat. "It *will* be all right," I said.

No answer. Just more tears.

"Where are you going to stay?"

He shrugged. "I don't know. I can't go to Saffron's. I can't go home. Mum and Dad hate me."

I said, "What about Anita's?"

He just looked at me, and I could see what he thought of that suggestion. Still, it *was* a pretty crap idea.

"What about Chris's?" I said. "He's got a sofa bed."

"Chris?" said Nick. "He hates my guts after Saturday."

"He doesn't hate your guts," I said. "Look, he's my mate. Once we tell him what's happened, he'll be fine about it. I'm sure he will."

My brother waited a long time before answering. At last, he said, "I suppose it's worth a try."

It was me who drove us there. I wasn't insured for Nick's car, but what the hell. This was kind of an emergency, wasn't it, and Nick was too upset to drive safely.

Nick waited in the car while I pressed Chris's buzzer.

"Yeah?" he said through the speaker. I was surprised he was in so early from the pub.

"Chris? It's Mark."

"What do you want?" He sounded well narked.

"Listen, mate, I've got a really big favour to ask."

"What? Look, I've got a bird with me."

I blushed, embarrassed. It wasn't going to be easy to get him to put Nick up for the night. I knew how rare it was for Chris to pull. "Is it all right if Nick spends the night at yours?" I said. "I wouldn't ask but he's desperate. His missus has kicked him out."

Chris laughed. "Seen the light, has she?"

"Chris, please. It's just for one night. And he'll keep out of your way."

"You must be joking. After what he tried to pull Saturday? Come on, Mark."

"Chris, he's desperate."

"No."

I lost my temper. "Why do you have to be such a wanker?" I shouted. "Can't you just think about someone other than yourself? Just for once?"

"Mark, I'm about to shag the most beautiful bit of stuff I'm ever likely to get my hands on, all right? I haven't got time to be pissing about with your sad excuse for a brother. I'll see you tomorrow."

But I wouldn't give up. "Come on, Chris. You're supposed to be my mate."

There was a massive pause; I thought he'd gone. But finally, "All right. But just for one night, yeah? And you owe me, Mark Holly. Big time."

I grinned. "Cheers, Chris. You're a real mate."

"Yeah, yeah," he said. "Send him up." Then he was gone.

I breathed a small sigh of relief, then turned and gave Nick the thumbs up. My brother leapt out of the car, bounding over with one of the sports bag. "It's all right?" he asked hopefully.

I nodded. "Just for one night, though. You'll have to get yourself sorted out for tomorrow."

Nick looked crestfallen then, but I said, "Look, I'll try and sort something out with Mum and Dad, yeah. Explain to them a bit more. I'll tell them your marriage was on the rocks. I don't know. I'll say Saffron's secretly a lesbian or something."

That made him laugh. It was good to hear it.

We both went up to Chris's flat, but stopped at the closed

door. "You coming in, too?" Nick asked.

I shook my head. "No. He's got a bird in, by the way. So don't say I didn't warn you."

Nick just looked blank. He was so miserable. I just wanted to wrap my arms around him, tell him it would be all right in the end. But of course I knew it wouldn't. He'd fucked things up good and proper.

"I'll see you later, yeah?" I told him.

He just nodded. I patted him awkwardly on the shoulder and hurried downstairs.

I walked for ages. It was freezing cold, but I could hardly feel it. I didn't know where to go. Not home, that was for sure. I didn't want to see Grace, since she was a part of it all. Chris was busy with his bird, and besides, Nick was there.

I went to the Lion and Eagle and had a pint. It cheered me up a bit, but not much. I checked my watch. It was seven o'clock. I wondered if Andrew was in. Probably not. He probably started work around now, and I didn't feel like heading down to Medusa's. Nevertheless, I decided to try his flat.

I got the bus there, surprised I'd remembered the way. I didn't have that good a head for places.

He was in. "Mark?" he said. He looked both surprised and pleased to see me.

"All right?"

"What are you doing here?"

I felt like an idiot. "Is it a bad time?" I asked. I wondered if he had a bloke with him, and – horribly – I actually felt a bit jealous.

But he shook his head. "No, no. Come in." He stood aside and I slipped into the flat. "Is something the matter?"

I looked at him. "What makes you say that?" He was wearing white jeans and a dark woolly jumper with a white stripe across the middle. He looked cool.

He shrugged. "You just seem a bit anxious."

I sighed. "It's my brother." I looked at the floor.

"What happened? Do you want a drink?"

"Yeah. Thanks, that'll be good."

He went through to the kitchen and I sat down on the sofa. He returned with a couple of Holsten Pils and as we drank

I told him all about it.

When I'd finished, he said, "That's rough."

"Yeah."

"You know, I'm no stranger to family troubles," said Andrew.

"No?"

He shook his head. "You should have been there when my mum found out I was gay. Talk about World War Three."

I was interested. "How old were you when you... you know... told her?"

"Nineteen. She found out by accident, actually. I'd gone to a gay pub, met this bloke, three years older than me, he was. And of course, muggins me, invites him round the next day, to my house. Things got... a bit heated between us."

"You ended up in bed together?" I asked, trying to ignore the hot feeling spreading through my groin.

Andrew nodded. He laughed, a little sadly. "Course, that's when my mum decides it's the perfect time to come home early from work and see if I needed any washing doing. She was a nurse, see, and I'd forgotten she was doing an early shift, instead of a late."

I actually gasped. "What did she do?"

"Just stood there. She stood there, mouth open. All she said was, 'When your father finds out about this...' and she just kept shaking her head. It was awful. It was the worst moment of my bloody life."

"I can imagine," I told him. The horror of it. I tried to picture what my old man would do if the same thing happened to me. The poor bastard'd have a stroke!

"So did your dad find out?" I said, needing to know the rest of the story.

Andrew shook his head. "Nope," he said. "Still doesn't know to this day. My mum had inherited this flat, you see, from her mum. She signed the lease over to me, said I could live here and live my life the way I wanted to. But she said if I stayed gay, that was it, I was no longer part of the family. That's a joke, isn't it? If I stayed gay. As if anybody has a choice."

I swallowed thickly, nervously. "She disowned you?"

"Yep." Again, he laughed sadly. "Dad's got a dodgy ticker.

She reckoned if he found out I was a 'filthy queer' as she called it, it'd do him in. So I went. I had no choice."

"Couldn't you have just pretended to be, you know, straight?" I asked, finding the story fascinating.

"Why should I?" he said, a bit affronted. "I'm gay, Mark, and there's no getting away from that. Why should I have to compromise my sexuality just to suit the needs of others? This is the nineties, after all."

I grinned. What courage Andrew had, to stand by his convictions, to give up his parents. "Have you got any brothers or sisters?" I asked.

He shook his head. "Just me. Maybe that's why Mum took it so badly, 'cos I was all she had. Still, at least I've got this flat. At least she didn't leave me homeless. I suppose that's something, isn't it?"

I nodded. But it was all so sad. I thought of Nick, wondering if Mum and Dad would do to him what Andrew's mother had done to *her* son.

I stood up. "Cheers for the drink," I said. "I'd better go."

"Stay a bit longer," he protested, as I started for the door. I put my hand on the front door handle and he put his hand on my shoulder, gently. I froze.

"No," I said, closing my eyes, like I was trying my hardest to resist something. "I have to go home, try and sort this out. Somehow."

He was silent for a moment, then, "Yeah. I suppose you have to. Life's too short, isn't it, to fall out with your family?" How sad he sounded, how remorseful. But he had courage, more courage than me, more than most people, of that I was sure. The choices he'd made, the choices he had to live with. It was really something to admire.

"'Bye, Andrew," I said. "You've been a good help."

"Any time, Mark," he told me. And I knew he meant it.

# 9

THE NEXT FEW days were pretty awful. Nick stayed at Chris's for two nights, but had to move out, his own choice. The girl Chris had met the other night, Gloria, had now become his girl-friend. They were at it every night, according to Nick, and he'd had enough of Chris's grunts of joy and Gloria's squeals of delight coming through the paper-thin walls.

Fortunately, Mum and Dad had agreed to take Nick back. He'd moved in to Amy's old room. It was good to have him home again, but don't ask me why since all he did was mope around in his jockeys, not shaving, not even washing. He didn't go to work, said he was too miserable because of the divorce papers Saffron had had slapped on him. Couldn't say I blamed him.

Surprisingly, Dad was sympathetic, though Mum was still a bit on the weepy side.

On Friday morning, while Nick was sitting in front of the TV, staring blankly at the Teletubbies, Dad came home from a job, sat down next to my brother and said, "Listen, son. We all make mistakes. Now it's time for you to face up to yours." Nick looked at him and started crying, Dad comforted him.

I couldn't believe it! Talk about speechless. I was just on my way out to the flat for yet more rehearsals as it was our second gig at Forbidden the next day.

Anita hadn't been in contact with us since Monday. I supposed she was still figuring out what to do with the baby. Part of me still held the hope that she'd get rid of it. Yeah, yeah, I know abortion is supposed to be really evil and wicked and sinful and all that jazz, but so is adultery.

Nick, a dad! Bizarre. Truly bizarre. But I kind of liked the idea of being an uncle. Uncle Mark. Has a nice ring to it, don't you think?

Anyway, Mum came up with this idea to invite Anita round for a meal on Sunday so they could all 'discuss the possibilities'. Already they'd written off Saffron and Nick. Been there, done that; it was all over as far as the Holly family were concerned. I reckoned it was pretty decent that my parents were finally being supportive of Nick. Better than Andrew's mum had been of her son, anyway.

I couldn't help but wonder if Anita would agree to the meal and, as it turned out, it was my job to ask Grace to ask her sister. Well, you can imagine what sort of position that put me in. Jesus, how I regretted that night in the Lion and Eagle when we'd come across those two. But, of course, if it hadn't been for Grace, I'd never've gone to Medusa's, and if I'd never gone to Medusa's, I'd never've met Andrew.

I know what you're thinking. Me? Pleased that I'd met Andrew? Never! But yeah, it was true, and it was all to do with what he'd told me the other day, about standing by his convictions, about not compromising his sexuality to suit the needs of others. He'd had to give up his whole family just because he was gay. What sacrifice. So it got me thinking. If I *was* gay, was it really the end of the world? After all, if Andrew could do it...

I called Grace and told her about the plan. She said it was a good idea and was sure Anita would attend.

Mum was on cloud nine, deciding what to make for the big dinner. It was like Nick had never been married. By about lunch time, my parents were saying things like "Well, I never really liked that Saffron, anyway," and "Bit too snotty for my liking; Nick's better off without her." It was unreal.

I rehearsed with the band as usual, told the lads what was going on round ours. They were really eager to know, like it had become a soap opera or something.

We wrote a new song about it, actually, called *Happy Accident*, and planned to play it the next day.

When I went home that night, Nick was on the phone to Anita. He was laughing. They were actually discussing baby names! Truthfully! But that's our family for you, we don't mess about.

How easily they'd accepted it all. It got me thinking. What would they say if I told them I was gay? Before, I'd have said they'd react in a similar way to Andrew's mum, but now... what with everything that had happened...

I shut the idea out of my head. I'm *not* gay, I told myself. So why even bother thinking about it?

We had kebabs for tea that night. Nick's favourite. Honestly, he goes out and knocks up another woman and look what he gets? Anyone'd think he'd won the lottery!

The next day I got up bright and early and took the bus to Chris's. I was well hyped about the gig, especially after last week. Grace said she'd be there, and she might even bring Anita with her. That made me feel good, you know, because at least it showed that Anita was all right. I felt really bad for her when Nick dumped her. And all that stuff Grace had told me, about her trying to do herself in, frightened the life out of me. I decided that Mum and Dad were right: Saffron was a bit too snotty – for my brother, anyway. Anita was much more his type, I decided, and since she was carrying his child that put the icing on the cake, didn't it?

We set our equipment up, had a couple of drinks courtesy of Ron and pretty soon the punters started to arrive. Grace didn't turn up until the third song, and as she'd said, she wasn't alone. Only it wasn't Anita standing beside her. It was Andrew.

I almost dropped my drumsticks. Andrew? At Forbidden? With my friends?

And then in the next instant, I thought, *So what? So what if he's here? He's a mate, ain't he?*

I grinned over at them both and continued to play my heart out. It was my best performance yet. I don't know whether that was because of Andrew being there. Looking back, it probably was, but at the time I kept that thought securely out of my head. Just concentrate on the music, I told myself. Forget everything but the music.

And it worked. By the end of the set, I was knackered, but grinning like mad.

I climbed out from behind the drums and bounded over to them, forgetting about the other lads. Grace kissed me. Andrew shook my hand. "Bloody excellent," he said.

"Even better than last week," Grace added.

She'd ordered me a pint and I drank half of it in one go. I was so high! Jason, Jim and Chris ambled over to us, all as chuffed as me. I felt a bit nervous, you know, about Andrew, but it was nowhere near as bad as I would've expected. I introduced him to the others, told them he was an old mate of mine who'd just moved down here. They all accepted this explanation completely. I don't know why, but I thought for some reason they wouldn't. Grace accepted it, too, even though she knew the truth. Yeah, she knew me pretty well already.

"I bumped into him downtown," she told me. "On his way to work. I didn't think you'd mind if I brought him."

"Course not," I told her, then to Andrew, "What about work?"

Andrew grinned. "I thought I deserved another night off," he said, and that made me feel brilliant.

To Grace, I said, "What about Anita?"

"She didn't fancy it. I think she's too wrapped up in Nick."

For a while we chatted, about the whole thing between my brother and her sister. Grace was pleased about it. This really amazed me, but it was good. The last thing I needed was hassle from her.

Little did I know that pretty soon my life would be nothing *but* hassle.

The evening was going nicely. Ron came over and said the audience reaction was better than last week, which made us all feel really stoked. Gloria turned up a little bit later, too, along with a few of her mates from the supermarket where she worked. We had quite a crowd there by about midnight; it was excellent. And what really made it for me was Andrew being there. The more I saw him, the more I liked him and even then it was getting beyond the 'just mates' stage, only sort of without me even noticing. We laughed together, drank beer, you know, the usual kind of crap lads get up to. He got on with the rest of my mates like a house on fire, like he'd always known them. But Andrew has that effect on people.

At one point, when everyone was laughing together, he said to me, "I've had a really good time tonight, Mark. Cheers for inviting me."

"I didn't invite you," I pointed out.

He just shrugged. "Whatever. It's been good. Your band – it's gonna be massive, I know it."

I grinned. "Cheers."

And then we just looked at each other, for only a split

second, but it felt like ages. His eyes seemed to be saying *I know that you know.*

I looked away, and just like that the spell was broken and we joined the group again.

We left Forbidden at about three o'clock, but the place was still jumping; it was that kind of club. Everyone split up then. Jim went home; Jason and Chris went off to have a curry with Gloria and a girl named Suze who Jason had had his eye on all evening. The other people who'd been hanging out with us just seemed to drift off on their own. I didn't know them, they were what you might call 'liggers'.

So all that was left was me, Grace and Andrew.

And the thing was, I wished Grace wasn't there.

"What now?" she said and I looked at Andrew. He was blank, as if his expression had been erased. The three of us stood there on the cold street, like we were waiting for something to happen, for some divine being to tell us what to do.

I looked at Grace again. I knew I should have gone home with her, made love to her. I'm sure that's what she wanted.

Only it wasn't what I wanted.

"I'd better call it a night," I said, faking a yawn but then Grace looked a bit put out so I quickly went on. "You know, we've got the big dinner tomorrow." I tried to laugh, but it came out all pathetic and shivery.

"Are you going to be there?" she asked.

"I don't know," I said. "We'll see. See what Mum wants."

Grace sighed. "Yeah, I guess you're right. I'd best be with Anita, too. She's dead nervous about tomorrow."

"I'll get off as well, then" said Andrew, who must have been feeling pretty left out.

Grace said, "Let's share a taxi, then. I mean, it's the logical thing to do."

So that's what we did. The pet shop was nearest, so we went there first. I kissed Grace on the mouth and she climbed out of the taxi. "See you tomorrow yeah?" I said.

She smiled, nodded. "You were brilliant tonight," she told me, and I had to look away, embarrassed. Andrew was beside me and I could sense he felt the same way.

Grace stood on the pavement, waving as the taxi pulled

away.

"Where to now then, lads?" the driver asked.

"Your flat," I told Andrew straight away, even though we were nearer to my house. Of course, Andrew didn't know that.

He shrugged, and told the driver the address.

Minutes later, we arrived. "I'll see you, Mark," he said, opening the door.

"I'm coming in with you," I said. "Might as well. Get a nightcap"

Andrew looked shocked, but I was more shocked. Then his lips curled into a smile and he shrugged. I didn't know what I was doing, but it felt right. Maybe it was the booze. Then again, maybe it wasn't.

I got out of the cab, paid the driver, watched it pull away. Andrew and I stood on the pavement for a while before going inside. We didn't speak. Didn't even look at each other. My head was so jumbled, with all kinds of conflicting feelings. I felt like I was standing at some sort of crossroads. The sexuality crossroads. Sounds like some sort of tacky late-night quiz show, doesn't it?

Andrew said, "Do you want to go in?" and his voice was very soft, very inviting. And yet it was tainted with something that sounded like fear.

I nodded. "Yeah. Bloody freezing out here."

We went up to the flat; Andrew made two cups of coffee. I had mine black, two sugars. I sipped it thoughtfully, looking at him. I don't think I was ready, but it was like my mind had gone off on its own.

Andrew said, "What did you really come up here for, Mark?"

The question threw me. I kept seeing those porn mag captions: *GAY VIRGIN TAKING HIS FIRST STIFF COCK. GAY GUYS WITH FAT COCKS SUCKING AND FUCKING EACH OTHER.* Remembering how hard I'd got. How hard I was getting now.

Andrew took a step towards me. I wanted to take a step back. But I didn't. Something kept me where I was.

He said, "You're beautiful."

And then I started trembling slightly. I sipped some of the coffee. Please, I was thinking. Please don't let this be true. I don't want to want this.

Andrew took the coffee cup from my hands and placed it on the table. It all seemed to be happening in slow motion. "It's nothing to be ashamed of," he said.

I was close to tears and Andrew looked away. "I need to know, Mark," he said, and this time there was real pain in his voice, real hurt. "I want you. I really want you. But if you're not interested... " He trailed off, looked at me, and now the hurt in his voice was mirrored in his eyes.

I kissed him.

The sense of everything taking place in slow motion melted away; now it all seemed speeded up. I'd kissed another man. It wasn't a deep kiss; just a quick peck. Andrew was so stunned. He just stood there, staring at me. And then he smiled, this great big cheesy grin that seemed to say, *Ah ha. I knew it.*

I thought *What have I done? What have I fucking done?*

Andrew put his hand on the back of my neck and pulled me against him and this time he kissed me, deeply, tenderly. It lasted less than thirty seconds before I pulled away, shaking. "Sorry," I said. "Sorry... I'm... sorry."

I turned, fumbled with the door handle, eventually got the door open and ran. Andrew called out after me, but I didn't stop, not even to catch the bus. I just ran and ran and ran, and when I got too knackered to run I walked. After a few minutes it began to rain and when I finally got home I was soaked and my side ached with the most enormous stitch.

I thundered upstairs, collapsed fully clothed into the shower and turned it on. Scalding water poured down on me, but I hardly even noticed. I felt dirty, contaminated. Oh, God, what had I done? I sobbed and sobbed until it ached, and then I just lay there, soaking wet and weeping and hating myself.

# 10

THE BIG MEAL on Sunday went pretty well. Anita and Nick – they seemed so happy, like they were married. It was clear that Saffron was well out of the picture. I think Mum and Dad were pleased, actually. Saffron had always made them feel a bit, you know, beneath her, although she'd always treated me all right.

Grace didn't come round, but I hadn't really expected her to. Besides, I was pleased she hadn't shown, I just didn't think I could face her.

I'd woken up at about six in the morning, soaking wet in the shower with all my clothes on. I had the worst hangover of my life but I staggered out, peeled off my wet clothes and went to bed naked. I couldn't stop shaking, thinking of that kiss...

And the worst thing was, I liked it. I liked the arousal, feeling Andrew's mouth pressed against mine, his hand on the nape of my neck...

It made me feel sick to think about it. Bad enough that I'd kissed another bloke. Even worse that I'd enjoyed it.

I was unusually quiet that Sunday, kept myself to myself, only spoke when I was spoken to. Twice Mum asked me what was wrong; twice I told her nothing. I couldn't stop thinking about Andrew. Every time his name entered my head I felt all hot and uncomfortable.

I went to bed early, having taken one of Mum's sleeping pills. I knew I'd never be able to sleep otherwise, so it was best not to chance it and end up laying awake for ages.

When I got up the next day, I still felt drowsy from the effects of the pill. I had to sign on at eleven o'clock and hadn't even filled in my 'Looking for Work' form. For those of you who haven't yet experienced the pleasures of the dole queue, the 'Looking for Work' form is this booklet you have to fill in with all the jobs you've applied for in the last fortnight. I hated having to do it. It was like saying to the government, *Look, I've been a good little boy. Please let me have some money.*

Of course, I never actually applied for any jobs, I just jotted down a few of the adverts from the local rag and it worked every time.

So that's how I spent my morning. It was good actually, to get away from the house, away from the band and just do something a bit different.

I tell you, when signing on looks like 'something a bit different' you know you're in trouble.

I was so depressed when I got in. I couldn't stop thinking

about Andrew, about that kiss. God, what I would've given to turn back time so that we never went to Medusa's that night. Okay, I'd spend the rest of my life in denial, but I'd be happy. Now everything was totally fucked up, in my head, in my life.

And I'd thought Nick had had it rough! Compared to me, he was on easy street.

I fixed myself a sandwich, ate it, and went straight round to Chris's. The rest of the band were there, trying out a new song. They were all pleased to see me, but I wondered what they'd say if they knew what Andrew and I had gotten up to after the gig.

It made me blush even to think about it. But I couldn't keep harping on about that. What's done was done.

We rehearsed as usual. I got right into it, every tiny part of my concentration was just poured into the music. The more I thought about that, the less I thought about Andrew. But you know how that goes, the more you try *not* to think about something, the more you end up thinking about it.

*Andrew*, I thought. *Oh, Andrew, what have you done to me?*

I went out every night that week. Sometimes with the lads, sometimes on my own. I visited strip bars, where the girls sit on your lap and rub you up. I stuck money in their cleavage, whistled at them with all the other perverts. And all the time I was thinking, *What are you doing here, Mark? You don't belong here. You belong with –*

But I wouldn't allow his name to fill my head.

Sometimes, I'd find myself thinking, *Maybe I'm bisexual. Maybe I swing both ways.* It was possible.

But I didn't feel the way about Grace that I felt about Andrew. Not even close.

The truth was I wanted to be gay. Yeah, I did. But it was like society wouldn't let me.

Chris had a copy of the *Sunday Sport* at Wednesday's rehearsals, and there was this advert in it. You know, for porn videos, imported from Holland. And – yeah, you guessed it, there were a load of gay videos advertised. *Queer Is Cool* read the heading, and below it there was this picture of one of the videos. And the description... God, I got so hard. There was all this stuff about

'Two eighteen-year old guys hand-relieving each other' and 'Loads of bum fun' and 'Kinky sessions of guy-2-guy masturbation', 'Hard gay sex performed on 18-19 year old guys'.

I couldn't stop thinking of Andrew. What would it be like to touch him? For him to touch me...?

I hadn't seen Grace since Saturday. I didn't want to; it was getting to the stage when every time I was with her I just felt guilty, like I was cheating on her. And I suppose I was really, cheating on her, I mean. Because even though I hadn't yet admitted my own sexuality to myself, of course it was there. When I was making love to Grace, I wanted to be making love to Andrew. I kept wondering what he looked like naked, how much he fancied me, if he was attracted to me – stuff like that. I even masturbated over him a few times, once in Chris's toilet, while the band were out in the living room drinking beer and having a laugh, none the wiser that I was getting my jollies by imagining a full sex romp with another man.

When Grace phoned, on Friday, I was dead off with her. She kept going on at me, was I still interested in her, why hadn't I phoned her, was I having an affair. It really pissed me off. I mean, if anything, Grace and I were nothing more than casual partners – if there was such a thing.

All I told her was that I was sorry, that I'd been busy with the band. I don't know if she bought the story, but to tell you the truth I couldn't care. I was so close, you see. So close to fully admitting I was gay. Before – you know, before Andrew had come along – I'd always shut the word away, made it seem unreal, that there was absolutely no way I could be bent. But now Andrew was there, and all those gay lads I'd seen at Medusa's, ordinary blokes, who just happened to be attracted to the same sex... It was like, big deal, you know? And did it mean that just because I was one of them it was some great and terrible sin? Of course not.

Well... at least, that's what one half of me thought. The other half was sickened by the idea that I might be homosexual. Every time I masturbated, I'd always find myself fantasising about Andrew, but as soon as I climaxed, he'd be gone from my head, replaced by Melinda Messenger, or some other page-three bird with big tits. It was like I was saying, *There, see? You weren't wanking over a bloke! It was good old Melinda all along!*

Talk about denial.

Anyway, back to Grace. It was during the same phone conversation that she told me that she and a few of her secretary mates had gone down to Medusa's for a bit of a booze-up. It was one of her colleagues' birthdays or something. Of course, Grace saw Andrew there and she told me he'd asked about me.

I was in shock. I just stood there in the hall, the telephone against my ear, mouth open. Grace was asking if I was all right; she thought I'd hung up. I was shitting bricks, I tell you, and Christ was *that* an understatement! Andrew? Asked about me? I wondered what he'd said, had he told her about the kiss, did he say he thought I could be gay? After all, I'd practically snogged the bloke.

But of course, Andrew would never have done that to me. I just wasn't thinking straight, too rattled... too guilt-stricken, I suppose.

He'd just asked how I was. But in the end that was just as bad, because it sent my thoughts on yet another homoerotic landslide.


The gig on Saturday went just as well as the other two. Thankfully, I'd managed to get Andrew out of my head. But I knew I had to find a way out of it all, all the confusion. But what? I hadn't spoken to the guy for a week, so it wasn't helping me by just not having any contact with him. I hadn't been to Medusa's, so that was out, too.

It was like that kiss had stuck to me, stuck his image in my head.

I had to see him, if nothing else I just had to tell him it was over. Even though nothing had really started.

I went there on Sunday. Nick had taken Anita to the pictures, Mum and Dad were having their usual afternoon doze, following the momentous Sunday roast. My sister Amy had come round, along with her husband Tim. Me and Amy had always got on well, which is a lot more than I can say for my brother-in-law. Oh, he's all right, I guess, he just has this way of getting up my nose. He's such a bloody weakling, honestly, you've never seen anything like it. Lets my sister boss him round something chronic. Mind you, that description puts Amy in a bad light, and you couldn't be more wrong. She's brilliant, is Amy.

It was about two when I got to Andrew's. I was sure he'd be in. I knocked sharply on the door without bothering to ring up from downstairs. He looked pleased to see me.

"Mark! How – "

But I cut him off. "We need to talk," I told him sternly. I was on a mission, see. There was neither the time nor the room for pleasantries. Besides, if I allowed him to squeeze by with all that, I knew we'd probably end up in bed together, the way my fantasies had been going.

He stepped aside and let me into the flat. The place smelt of him and my heart raced. A vision of the two of us in the shower together flashed through my mind, all soapy together, hands going where they shouldn't...

I sliced off the fantasy. Now wasn't the time.

Andrew said, "What's up? You want a beer or something?"

I shook my head. "It's about us."

"Us?" He seemed truly confused.

"Yeah, us. That kiss... last week. Remember?"

"Oh." That's all he said. *Oh.* Can you believe it? But his eyes went all distant, as if he were about to cry. He knew, you see. He knew right then, I'm sure, that I was gay. I realised after that he probably thought I'd come round to tell all, to confess about the way I felt.

It must have broken his heart when I said what I did.

I just blurted it all out. "I'm not gay, Andrew. I'm not. The other night... I'd been drinking. Or something. Too many ideas in my head. I'm not gay, though. I don't fancy men, I fancy women. And I'd appreciate it if you'd stop asking people about me. I'm sorry if you're attracted to me, but I'm just not gay."

And then I walked out. Didn't wait for a reaction from him – nothing.

Of course, I hated myself for it. But what else could I have done?

Three weeks went by and I didn't see Andrew. I tried as best I could to forget about him. It wasn't easy, mind, but I had to manage it. The band was going great. We'd played our regular Saturday night spot at Forbidden, as well as two other slots on Fridays and Wednesdays. Ron said we were making the profits for the place soar, so of course he wanted us to be there more and more. We were getting quite a following, actually. There were these three girls, couldn't have been more than eighteen, who LOVED us. They were always there, always pushing these little notes into our hands. Gloria didn't take too kindly to them; she didn't want Chris to be with anyone else and was convinced that the time he didn't spend with her he was shafting every female fan in sight. Paranoid? Deranged more like it.

Things with me and Grace were on a pretty even keel, I suppose. I hadn't slept with her for almost a month, though. I didn't want to betray her, and in a way that's what I was doing. Because of Andrew.

She was starting to get suspicious, I knew. Of course, she didn't exactly say this, but I could tell it was true. Maybe part of me wanted her to find out I was secretly gay, maybe, subconsciously, that's what I was trying to do, spare me the bother of coming out on my own.

But I was a fool to think it could be that easy, and in the back of my mind, Andrew was always there. When I was playing in the band. When I was at home, watching telly. When I was eating. Always there.

And so was that kiss.

Three weeks I'd been away from him. Twenty-one days. Not much, but it felt like forever.

I couldn't go back there, though. I couldn't!

I spent my time carefully, using my concentration up on everything. Taking a shower, cleaning my teeth, writing a song. I had to divide my attention so precisely, allotting some to everything but Andrew.

*Andrew.* His name crept into my head even as I tried to fight it. *Andrew.*

I started to resent my family. I used to spend all my time up in my room, only coming down for meals. I was more quiet than usual, and my parents and brother wasted no time picking up on this.

"What's up with you?" they'd ask.

And I'd go, "Nothing. I'm just a bit tired, that's all." It was an excuse they'd easily believe, knowing how hard I worked on the band.

Chris reckoned it wouldn't be long before we were spotted, you know, by a talent scout or something, or an A & R man. We'd received a few rejection letters from companies, concerning our demo disc, but we weren't that put out. I mean, there are thousands of hopefuls out there, all sending off their little home-made tapes and CDs and after a while the people who listen to them can't tell one from the other and that's how you end up losing a major talent. If you wanted to make a real impression, you had to be seen live.

But I couldn't concentrate on all that, I could only concentrate on one thing.

And you *know* what that is.

In the end, I couldn't stand it anymore. I'd cracked. I had to see Andrew. I was half-way there, see, to admitting the truth to myself. That's the hardest part. Once that's out, all you have to do is tell the ones you love. Easy, eh?

Yeah, sure.

I think it was an accident, though. No, not me being gay, but going to see Andrew that night. It was a Thursday evening. I had nothing to do. Grace had gone up West with Anita and a few pals; Chris was working; Jason and Jim were off somewhere doing their own thing; Nick was working; Mum and Dad had gone down the pub. I was alone in the house, with a bottle of vodka. I'd turned to drinking quite heavily recently. Sad, isn't it? But it made me feel better, and that's just what I needed. At the end of the day, isn't that what everybody needs? To feel better?

I walked the full distance to Andrew's flat, staggering slightly, the bottle in my hand. I must have looked like an old drunk. I felt like I was on my way to a show-down, pistols at dawn or something. But I was determined. Tonight, I told myself, something is going to happen.

I was at those sexuality crossroads again. My heart telling me one thing, my head another. A cliché, I know, but that's what my life felt like. One big cliché.

I went straight up to the flat, knocked on the door. It opened slowly and as soon as I saw Andrew, I sobered up. It was like magic. One minute pissed as a fart, the next...

"Hi," he said, in a small voice.

I swallowed before answering. Finally, I muttered, "Hello."
I was so nervous.

"Er, come in," he said, and I saw immediately that he was
just as nervous. He was wearing dark blue pyjama bottoms and
a white T-shirt.

I went into the flat, feeling horribly shaky but then, in a
lightning-quick instant, a sort of courage spread through me.
*This is it*, I told myself. *No going back.*

Andrew said, "Erm, what can I do for you?"

I thought, *He is so handsome.*

I couldn't meet his eyes. "I wanted to apologise," I said.
"For that night."

"Oh."

There was a long silence. At last I looked at him and then
out it all came. "I'm sorry, Andrew. You were right. I'm gay.
I'm a fucking gay." And then I just broke down in a flood of
tears.

## 11

FOR JUST A moment time seemed to stand still. I stopped crying
and just looked down at the carpet. I couldn't meet his eyes, I
couldn't. Still, it felt good that the truth was out. It was like
giving birth, I reckon. It hurts and hurts and hurts while you try
to push it out, but once you've done it, there's this tremendous
sense of relief.

The atmosphere in the room was heavy, as if the truth had
substance, as if the truth were some third party, an actual figure
taking up space.

Finally, after what seemed like a lifetime, I raised my eyes
to Andrew's. He was standing over me, smiling. It was a good,
affectionate smile. Not a *Now you're arse is mine* smile.

"You okay?" he said gently.

I got to my feet, the vodka bottle still in my hand. "Yeah,"
I said, wiping away the tears. "Erm, sorry. I have to go."

"Sit down, Mark," Andrew said, like a teacher. "We need

to talk, don't we? *You* need to talk."

I just stared at him pathetically.

He shook his head. "You can't keep running away from it, Mark. No one can outrun the truth. It always catches up with you in the end."

He was right. Oh, how right he *was.* It had. You could run and run to the ends of the earth, just like I'd run from Andrew's flat twice before. Only the thing was I *wasn't* running away from Andrew, not really. I was running away from myself, from the facts I'd hidden away from even my own mind.

He sat down next to me and put an arm around my shoulders. Even his touch was enough to excite me, which was a lot more than Grace was able to do.

"It's all right to be gay, Mark," he said, and his voice was as soft as a lullaby. "There's no shame in it. Not any more."

I started to weep. "But... I don't want to be gay."

"Nobody does. Nobody *wants* to be gay. They just are."

I looked at him. "You knew, didn't you? You knew I was gay."

He nodded.

"How...?"

"I just did," he said. "I could see you were confused. It was practically written all over your face that night at Medusa's. All that macho crap. 'I'm not gay, honest'."

I laughed. But then cringed. Had I been that obvious around everyone?

"Relax," said Andrew, as if he'd read my last thought. "I can tell, because *I'm* gay. It's not obvious to everyone."

I thought, *Oh, good. So the whole gay community could tell I was... one of them.*

"When did you decide to tell me?" said Andrew.

"About ten seconds ago. I tried to tell myself I wasn't gay, that's why I haven't been here for the past month. Every time I saw you I got more and more convinced, and I didn't want it. I wanted nothing to do with it."

Andrew just looked at me and I kissed him again, not just a peck this time, but a full kiss. It felt good. It was real this time, I wanted it, and I knew I wanted it. I was feeling so high, lighter than light. It was freedom, this new feeling, it was liberation.

Andrew stroked my face as we pulled apart. "You sure this is what you want?" he asked and I just nodded, and kissed him again.

Now I don't want to go all Mills and Boon on you here. You've probably worked out by now that this isn't your every-day love story, boy meets boy and all that crap. But it is important to mention that this wasn't some kinky sex thing we had going that first night, it was more like an exploration of one another, if that doesn't sound too weird.

I stayed the night, but we didn't have sex. We went into his bedroom, kissed some more and stripped off, keeping our eyes locked on one another's. We hugged, we stroked, we kissed. But we didn't have full sex. I don't think I was ready. He just ran his hands over my chest, my genitals, gently fondling, kissing my mouth. It was erotic, so much more... real, I suppose the word is, than anything I'd shared with a woman. I guess you have to actually be gay to know what I'm talking about. The first time a homosexual is intimate with another man, particularly if you've been living in denial as I had been, it's just so... I dunno... breathtaking

That night, beside Andrew, I'd never slept better.


*I have to get out of here.*

That was my first thought when I woke up. I turned over and saw him, propped up on one elbow, smiling at me with that dreamy look in his eyes. He had two tattoos on his upper arm: the Japanese symbols for Tiger and Dragon, he explained. They looked brilliant.

"Morning," he said and I smiled, and the thought of leaving turned cold and vanished. I was happy where I was, thank you very much. He kissed me and ran a hand down my arm. I just closed my eyes and let him do what he wanted. It felt fucking wonderful. "You still okay?" he asked and there was this look in his eyes that said, *Please don't leave me. Don't tell me you've changed your mind.*

But I said, "Never better," which made him kiss me again. I looked at the alarm clock and saw that I was late for rehearsals.

"I have to go," I said and I got out of the double bed and pulled on my clothes.

"Not again," said Andrew, looking worried. "Mark, I thought we went through this, there's nothing wrong with – "

I cut him off. "I'm late for rehearsals," I explained. "Chris'll kill me." And then it occurred to me that nobody knew where I was, not my family, my band, or Grace. "Shit!" I said. "They'll be worried sick."

"You're a big boy now," said Andrew smiling.

"Don't be a smart arse."

I left the flat and got a taxi to rehearsals, instead of the bus. I was on top of the bloody world! I wanted to scream and shout: *I did it! I slept with a bloke! And you know what? I don't give a shit! I'm free, gay and happy!*

As it turned out, I was only ten minutes late and didn't even get shouted at. As a matter of fact, Chris had some good news and as Jason let me in, I caught the tail end of what he was saying.

"...more money, so I said yeah, why not?"

"What's more money?" I asked.

The fat singer turned to me, cheeks as red as cherries. "We've got a special gig lined up for Saturday."

"At Forbidden?" I asked.

Chris shook his head. "Forget Forbidden, mate. Medusa's is offering us *twice* what we get at the dump. I know, I know, it's a gay club, but hey, money's money, and exposure is exposure. We've got to broaden our horizons, see?"

I felt sick. Medusa's? Again? And even worse – a gig! It was all I could do not to scream and immediately my thoughts turned to Andrew. I mean, what if he thought that now we'd slept together, now that I'd admitted how I felt, what if he thought I was going to tell everyone? What if he tried something at the gig? Let slip to the others that I was gay?

I tried to keep calm, but it wasn't easy.

"Brilliant," I said, hoping it sounded enthusiastic, which of course it didn't.

We rehearsed until it hurt. When I got home later that night, Mum was instantly on my case with her "What happened to you last night?" and "There's such a thing as a telephone, you know". Blah, blah, blah...

Again, excuses were easy. "I went round an old school mate's," I said. "Flat- warming party. Got a bit bladdered. Sorry I didn't phone."

Of course, she believed it.

At about nine, I went round to Andrew's. I told my parents I was visiting the same mate and they were fine about it.

He was pleased to see me, greeting me with a kiss. I told him about the gig at Medusa's. I'm not sure why, but I was expecting him to make some kind of fuss. I told him that the others were not, *not, NOT* to know about me being gay. He was a bit hurt, actually, that I'd suspected he might tell them. Of course he knew it was difficult; after all, he'd been in the same situation before, hadn't he?

I didn't stay there that night, though we did kiss a lot. We drank lagers, chatted about silly, trivial things. But the atmosphere was so much more relaxed now that I'd admitted my sexuality. I felt like I owned the world, though I have to admit I felt more than just a touch guilty over the way I'd asked Andrew not to reveal how we'd slept together. It was mean and low-minded, I guess, to think he'd betray me. *Of course* he wouldn't tell.

I left his place at about eleven that night. We kissed again, and hugged, and I could feel through his jeans how hard he was. *I did that*, I told myself, and the rush of adrenaline came like you wouldn't believe. I knew I was almost ready for it – you know, full gay sex. The thought of Andrew doing it to me sent my fantasies soaring higher than ever.

Maybe that sounds smutty, I don't know. But that's how I felt. Now that I was free from my own denial, there was no stopping me.

I mean, this isn't meant to be all lovey dovey, hearts and flowers and all that crap. That doesn't happen in real life. In real life, couples want sex, sex and more sex. It's no different for gay men, you know, we still have the same fantasies, the same appetites.

Andrew said he couldn't wait to introduce me to the full pleasures of rear sex. That made me nervous, to be honest, but I still wanted it. You wouldn't believe how much.

94

Saturday arrived and we – the band – were raring to go. I was looking forward to the Medusa's gig now; Andrew would be my inspiration for the entire set. He was working that night, but it didn't bother me. At least he'd be there. That was the main thing, as far as I was concerned.

You're probably thinking how quickly the whole transformation has taken place, that only a little while ago I was all but homophobic and now I'm a fully-fledged gay. But that's what it's like, the self-discovery. It *does* happen that quickly. One minute you're trying to kid yourself that fancying other men is disgusting, the next you're loving every minute of it. Mad... but true.

We drove to Medusa's in Chris's van at about five o'clock. I got a little nervous during the journey to the night-club 'cos the lads were making all sorts of anti-gay comments, you know the kind: *Don't bend down in the bogs, boys. Anyone of those perverts tries to buy you a drink smash their fucking queer heads in.*

I couldn't help wondering what they'd say if they knew about me, that I was one of those 'perverts'.

Just like Forbidden, Medusa's looked weird in the daylight, kind of like a ghost train with the lights turned on. There weren't many people there, just a few of the bartenders. Well, of course they didn't look gay, and Chris even said, "Blimey, they've even got normal fellas working here," to which I responded, "What did you expect? A load of drag queens in leopard-skin hot pants and stilettos mincing away to the Spice Girls?"

Andrew hadn't turned up yet and I can't deny I was disappointed.

We rattled off a couple of numbers for a sound check and were flawless. I knew they were going to love us.

The punters started to arrive and straight away we launched into our set. Sure enough the dance floor got crowded almost at once. Chris was really getting into it, which was a surprise to me at least. I'd expected him to be quite introverted during the performance, knowing what a devout homophobe he was.

Andrew arrived about an hour after our first song. He grinned at me, and I grinned back. The music had taken over, erasing any stupid worries or fears of discovery. I was free as a bird when I was playing my drums, no barriers, no lines. I was Mark Holly, a twenty-year-old gay man, and I loved it.

Our final song was *Tribal Sex*, which got the biggest applause. The crowd were much more appreciative than the one at Forbidden and I beamed with pleasure at Andrew, who was standing by the bar, empty glasses in hand. He winked at me, and that wink set my heart on fire. I couldn't wait for the gig to be over so we could go back to his flat, back to his bed...

"Cheers," Chris told the crowd. "You're the best." And it sounded like he meant it.

We climbed off the stage and made our way to the bar. Nick was there, along with Anita, his arm around her. "All right!" he said, wrapping a playful arm around my shoulder. "Bloody amazing again, bruv! Let me get you a drink." He got me and the rest of the lads a pint, but all the same kept his hand locked with Anita's. Obviously he thought he was sending out signals to all the gays around. *Make a pass at me and you're fucking dead you dirty fuckers.*

I frowned while I drank my pint, hoping that Andrew would know enough to keep his distance, at least for the time being.

I studied my brother, laughing with the boys, keeping each other enclosed in the safety of their heterosexual gathering.

And then it hit me. *They were afraid. They were afraid of gays.* I could see it in their eyes, the nervous glances. How paranoid they were.

I thought, *What would Nick do if he knew? What would he say?*

And the answer turned my blood to ice.

I managed to slip away an hour later, claiming I was tired. Andrew was waiting outside, leaning against the wall. Tonight he was wearing a black bomber jacket, his hair swept away from his face. I knew for a fact that his shift didn't finish for at least another hour. I'd been planning to go home, have a shower and meet him at his flat when he was done. But here he was, large as life. I said, "What are you doing here?"

He shrugged. "Had my shift shortened, didn't I?"

The pleasure of it. I grinned. "You got your car?"

"Yep."

"Let's go then."

We went. Back to his flat. Into his bed.

It was the greatest, most exciting moment of my life. There were no nerves, no fumbling. Andrew was so gentle, so tender as he touched me, as he entered me. I wanted to go for it, the hard stuff. All right, all right. I realise this sounds as if it's in danger of turning into some sleazy porn thing, but it's isn't, honest. I want to say how good it was, the sex. Okay, so it was painful... at first. But there was an amazing kind of bliss to it. Just the feel of him going inside me...

He gave me what I wanted, *whatever* I wanted. We gave each other hand-relief, oral sex, rear sex – the works. He came in my mouth; I came in his. Of course, we did it safely, condoms and lube and everything, but even so...

It was just like the stuff advertised in that video I'd mentioned earlier. I mean, yeah, part of it was dirty and raunchy, but it's just the same with straight sex, right? Everyone wants a bit of filth in their love lives, a bit of hardcore porn. And on that night, that's just what I wanted.

It was, literally, fucking amazing.


## 12


ANOTHER WEEK WENT by. It was a pretty bland week, filled with endless rehearsals. Ron had dropped us from the Forbidden line-up. He was pissed off that we'd played Medusa's and as a result had got a new group in, some sad indie outfit called the Secret Shrimps. Of course, they were total shite, not a patch on Lyar, but what could we do? If Ron Donn (yeah, I promise you, that was his last name) wanted to make the biggest mistake of his life by letting us go, that was his problem.

Still, things were on the up and up for us. "We don't need a gig at that dive anymore," Chris said.

Medusa's had booked us in for another Saturday, and we had the word that a talent scout for one of the country's leading independent record labels would be there, having been tipped off about us. This was great news, not just because the bloke would be there – we could have asked someone to see us ages ago. But to think he'd been tipped off! Imagine, someone else had actually recommended he check us out. It was like a dream, I'm telling you.

During those seven days, I regularly saw Andrew. We had to meet in secret, of course, or at his flat, but there's always a price to pay. With everything in life, there's always a price.

Andrew was the first bloke I told about the talent scout. He was stoked for me, naturally, and we celebrated the arrangement by having more hot sex.

There was no doubt about the fact I was feeling more relaxed about my sexuality, so much so that it had reached a new degree. I didn't want it to all be a big secret anymore. Andrew and I had the best time in bed, but by now it wasn't just about sex. It was about love. I loved him, and I knew he loved me, he told me so on a regular basis. I wanted my family to know about him, to take him home to meet my parents, to be able to hold his hand in the streets. Bottom line: I didn't want to have to close my feelings away behind the doors of his flat.

But how could I not? What other choice was there? It would be hard enough for the most relaxed family to accept that their son was homosexual, but mine? The people who think gay men should have done to them what Hitler did to the Jews? My dad? My mum? My brother? You've got to be joking.

It was torture, that, having to act all innocent in front of them. And then there was Grace. I hardly ever saw her, never phoned her. She was the one who always called me, and even then I always made up some excuse. Oh, I loved her, of course I did, she was probably my best friend. But sexually, there was nothing there. Not really. Just because I'd had sex with her, didn't mean I was straight. All that was forced, all those nights when we'd made love, I could see that now. Because with Andrew, sex reached new levels, it was a different kind of pleasure to straight sex; a *better* pleasure.

Things were getting so hot between us, I tell you. And the day he came round to my place... I couldn't resist. Everyone was out, I had the house to myself, and Andrew turns up, all casual in his black jacket, jumper and blue jeans. I couldn't believe he was actually there – and even better, I couldn't believe how much my luck was in. An empty house for me... and there was my boyfriend on the doorstep!

We went upstairs, to my room, and that was it. We were tearing at each other's clothes – couldn't strip fast enough. He'd bought these flavoured condoms round and we slipped them on and took turns sucking. Then it was more rear sex. It was the first time I did it to him. I was nervous, obviously, but he said I was nothing short of excellent, which made me blush.

We only did it a couple of times, though. We didn't mean to fall asleep, really we didn't. But we'd been going at it so hot and heavy that... well, I guess we were exhausted.

I mean, how was I to know my sister was going to walk in and find us?

It was like this little gasp, that turned into an "Oh my God!" It was only quiet, nothing more than a whisper. But it woke me up all right. I just shot up, which made Andrew begin to stir. I could feel his nakedness next to me and even though my sister was standing there, mouth open, this massive erection started to grow.

"Whu?" Andrew was saying beside me.

"Amy!" I blurted. She couldn't move. She had her hand over her mouth, her eyes were bulging. I felt like the world was about to end. The nightmare had happened.

All these scenarios started to run through my head, what my mum was going to say, my dad. I saw myself broken and beaten and bruised, lying in some swamp somewhere after I'd been murdered by my family.

And then Amy said, "How very modern," which struck me as the oddest thing in the world. And then she started to laugh, these really hysterical giggles.

I tried to think of some kind of excuse, something to get me out of the awful moment, but there was none. I was in bed with a naked man. Nothing I could say to her would hide the truth.

"Amy, please... " I trailed off.

But she just grinned and I thought, *Don't have a fit or anything.*

Then she goes, "My own brother. My own brother's gay.

That's a turn-up for the books, isn't it?" Her voice was calm. Relaxed. She seemed happy with what was happening, almost amused. I could only look at her. So could Andrew. He didn't say anything, either.

"Are you all right?" I asked my sister.

She grinned. "My own brother's gay," she repeated.

And I said slowly, "Yes. Does... it bother you?"

She just shrugged. "I guess not. So long as you keep your hands off Tim, I'm fine about it."

Well, I had to laugh about that. Tim? You gotta be kidding. I'd rather get off with Chris.

"No, you're all right there," I told her.

And she said, "Why, what's wrong with him?" but she was smiling as she said it. "I'll leave you to it," she added, and then she just turned and walked out of the room.

"Wow," said Andrew, half-awake.

"Do you believe that?" I whispered. But, oh, the joy of it.

"Would you mind if I went down to talk to her?" I said.

He shook his head. "No, not at all."

So I climbed out of bed and slipped into my towelling bath robe. I padded downstairs in my bare feet to find Amy in the kitchen, making herself a cup of coffee. I couldn't get over how easily she was accepting it all. At one point I even thought, *Am I dreaming this, or what?*

"Amy?" I said cautiously. "You sure you're all right?"

She turned and I half-expected her to be crying floods, but she was just her usual self. "I'm fine," she said. "Just in a bit of shock, I suppose. It's not every day you find out your brother's gay, is it?" And then she laughed, and the laugh came out sounding whole and genuine. I think I was more in a state of shock than she was, actually.

But then the mood changed, and she looked at me with eyes full of severity. "But listen, Mark," she said, like an oracle about to predict some great disaster, "I have no problem with you being gay. Absolutely no problem. In fact if I'm honest, I think I always knew. But don't tell Mum and Dad, okay? Please. It'll finish them. You know what they're like. You saw what happened with Nick."

I nodded solemnly. I knew what she said was right, of course

I did, but it sort of made everything final. Because I knew then that my stupid fantasies about my parents meeting Andrew, about my family accepting the way I was – it was all just dumb; naive.

"Will you promise me that, Mark?" she said.

"Of course," I told her. "I won't say a word."

She smiled. "Good," she said, and then she hugged me. "I have to say, though, you ain't half got good taste in men."

All I could do was laugh.

But things didn't get easier; they got harder. Another week passed, full of the same old routine. Playing in the band, playing at Medusa's. Andrew was all I could think about, and now that Amy knew, some of the torture about keeping everything under wraps was starting to ease. But it wasn't completely gone – I didn't think it ever would be.

Some nights I'd lie awake, wishing for a perfect world, without prejudice, without discrimination. Some joke. The whole of society was against me, and it was a horrible, cruel society. A free country? Yeah, right. What a fucking joke. There's no such thing as a free country, not in my book. In a free country, men could be with men without the fear of being disowned by their families, or having the living crap kicked out of them. In a free country, I'd be able to walk down the road, linking arms with my male lover.

This ain't a free country. Not to me. It's like a prison, a prison without walls, but with invisible boundaries. It made me feel sick to think what people's opinions of me would be if they knew the truth, if I came out.

Sometimes I nearly did. I got so close to the edge. Sitting at home, with my parents, watching television, I'd keep glancing over at them, wondering, Should I tell them now? What would they say? How should I approach the matter?

By the way, folks, your darling son is bent as a nine-bob note. Forgive me? Still love me?

Nice idea, right? I could just see how the old fella'd take that.

So when things got to that stage, I'd just go round to Andrew's and we'd talk it out. It was getting harder and harder to spend the night though, something that really bugged me. I kept having to come up with these explanations and my ideas were getting few and far between. The 'old school mate' story would only stretch so far, I knew, which meant my only choice was to come home every evening. I hated to leave Andrew, but there was no other way to go.

Until one evening, he dropped a major bombshell: "Why don't you just tell them?"

I was stunned. "WHAT?" I cried, unable to believe the crazy suggestion. "Are you mad? You know what would happen. Besides," I added, remembering Amy's plea, "I promised my sister I wouldn't."

This just made Andrew sigh and then very slowly, he said, "Mark. Whose life is this, eh? Yours or your sister's? You're gay. You've admitted it to yourself. Now you have to admit it to your family."

I was just about to blurt out, *Easy for you to say*. But Andrew had been there, done it, had the T-shirt. I remembered what he'd told me all those weeks ago, when his mum found him in bed with a man.

Why should I have to compromise my sexuality just to suit the needs of others?

Half of me agreed. Oh, how I wanted to agree! Totally, not just partially.

But then *his* Mum had found out by accident. Who's to say that if she hadn't walked into that bedroom and found him with that bloke Andrew would be here? He might still be living at home and his family would have been none the wiser.

He slid up to me and put his hands between my legs, gently rubbing me. "You are who you are, Mark," he said, and he kissed me, long and deep and hard, all the while rubbing me up. I climaxed a few seconds later, gasping, breathless with ecstasy.

"All right," I said, eyes closed. "All right. I'll tell them."

I was actually going to do it. I was ACTUALLY going to do it!

I stayed at Andrew's that night. It was a Wednesday, just three days before our big gig at Medusa's with the talent scout watching.

The next day I got up late, showered, shaved, dressed and took a taxi back home. It was about mid-day when I arrived. I was supposed to be in rehearsals, but I just thought, *Fuck it.* I had more important things on my mind. I'd hardly slept the night before, too busy thinking. I was going to tell them. I really was. Last night, while Andrew and I had been together, I'd agreed to it, but I couldn't help wondering if the next morning I'd change my mind, if maybe I'd chicken out, or decide the time wasn't right after all.

Then I realised there never would be a right time. For fuck's sake, I was twenty years old! Andrew was right. It was *my* life, not Amy's, although that fact did nothing to prevent me from feeling guilty. But still...

I knocked on the front door, though I had my key. Why I did this, I have no idea. It just seemed right. Maybe I'd already resigned myself to the idea of being different, of being a stranger, no longer belonging.

Mum answered and we went through the whole rigmarole of "Where have you been?", "How selfish are you?", Blah, blah, whatever...

I just went straight through to the living room, carefully concentrating on not thinking too much about what I was going to do.

And just my luck, Nick, Anita, Amy and Tim were there, too. They'd all popped round at the same time, by coincidence.

I thought, *Dear God, why do you mock me?*

But perhaps it was just as well. Perhaps it was best that I got it all over in one blow.

"I've got something to say," I began, and they all looked at me with curiosity. Except Amy. She looked ready to kill me, obviously knowing what the announcement was going to be.

My mum frowned. "What, love?"

My dad said, with a grin, "He and Grace are getting married, I bet!"

I swallowed thickly. The room was heavy with waiting. "No, Dad," I said, very slowly, very carefully. "It's not that."

"Then what is it?" This from Nick.

I stared at them all. "I'm gay," I said.

*Part Two*

# Nick

IT WAS LIKE a video that had been put on pause. We all just sat there, staring at Mark. He was bright red, and I thought, *This is a joke. This is some kind of sick-arse joke.*

We were all still for a few minutes, and then Mum laughed, this weird, flutey laugh. It was as if she *had* to laugh, or else she'd cry.

Dad was frozen to his chair, his face like a mask.

Under her breath, Amy muttered, "Shit."

Tim and Anita were just blank, stunned into silence.

And me? I couldn't do anything. I felt so sick, my insides all knotted up. But at last I said, "You're a liar," and Mark just looked at me with such sadness in his eyes and that was when it really hit me.

*He was telling the truth.*

I wanted to throw up. My own brother... queer? A fucking poofter? It was like some mad, bizarre nightmare. I couldn't get my head round it.

"Dad?" he said. "Say something."

I held my breath, too stunned to speak. Christ, what was the old man going to do? It was like waiting for an explosion, an eruption. He was going to go spare, I knew it. But it wasn't like that, not yet. He just turned his head very slightly and then in this odd, quiet voice I'd never heard him use before, said, "Tell me it isn't true, Mark. Please."

We all looked at my brother, and I'm sure we were all thinking the same thing. *Tell us it isn't true, Mark.*

He was quiet for ages, and for a second I thought he was actually going to burst into laughter, and start shouting, "Ha! You suckers! Had you going there for a minute, didn't I?"

But he didn't say it. No, he said, "I'm sorry. I can't."

Well, that did it for me. I got to my feet. "You filthy little fucker," I hissed at him. "You disgusting little shit."

Anita put her hand on my arm. "Nick, please... " she said, trying to make me calm down. But I was too wild to calm down. The full force of my little brother's confession slammed into my gut like a sledge-hammer. I was winded by it, but at the same time fuelled by rage. Mum was really crying now, her head in her hands and Dad was just sitting there, looking at the floor, like he didn't know what to do. I thought that any minute he'd start clutching at his heart and we'd end up having to call an ambulance.

Actually, make that two ambulances. One for Dad, one for Mark, 'cos believe you me, once I'd finished with him he'd need a damn ambulance.

I said, "You make me fucking sick." My fists were shaking.

"Nick, I can't help it," he said, his voice all quivery. He wasn't crying yet, but he was close to it.

Anita stood next to me. "You better go, Mark," she said. "I think that'd be a pretty wise move."

"Damn right," I said. "And never come back."

But he didn't go. "At least let me explain," he said, and then I just saw red. I punched him right on the jaw, with my full force. I'd never done that, not to anyone, not with my total strength, which is pretty massive, even if I do say so myself.

He reeled backwards against the wall and I punched him again, square in the face. I could actually feel his nose break and this time he went down. "Get up," I said, and now I was crying as well. "Get up, you filthy poof!"

He just looked at me, like a beggar or a slave. "Please don't do this," he said, his face all bloody. I went to kick him, I was so angry, but then Tim was behind me, holding me back.

"Leave it, Nick," he said. "This isn't going to solve anything, is it?"

"Piss off!" I shouted. "It might not solve anything, but it'll make me feel a hell of a lot better." I looked down at Mark. "Get up, you dirty queer! Get up and take your fucking medicine!"

And then Amy was there, too, and Anita, all trying to stop me from killing my brother.

"Nick, please," they kept saying. "Stop this."

I started sobbing. "How could he do it?" I said. "How could he do it to us?"

To Mark, who was now cowering, Amy said stonily, "Just go, Mark. Just go," and he staggered to his feet and lurched from the room, broken and bruised and bloody. I can't remember him actually leaving, I was too upset. The idea that my brother was bent... God, you have no idea what it was like. I felt crushed, sickened. All these scenes were flashing through my head of my little brother in bed with another bloke, being shagged up the arse, squealing like a stuck pig. I thought of AIDS and young guys dying in their twenties, because they can't be normal, they have to be perverted freaks.

It was awful.

Yeah, yeah, I know what you're thinking. Homophobic bigot. Well, that's just how I'd been raised, you know, that it's filthy and disgusting for blokes to get it on with other blokes. The thing was, Mark had been raised exactly the same way.

So why? Why him? Why did *my* little brother have to be one of those sickos?

I don't know the answer to that question, I don't think I even *want* to know.

Once Mark had gone, we just sat there in silence. Dad was trying to comfort Mum, who'd gone into tear overdrive. His face was like chalk. "Dad?" I said, sniffling, wiping my own tears away. The others just stood around like shop dummies. Nobody knew what to say.

Except Dad. He said, "I never want to see that filthy bastard again."

# Andrew

HE LOOKED LIKE he'd been run over by a car. His nose was smashed, his face already swollen. I felt sick, knowing what must have happened, knowing that it was me who'd put the idea into his head.

He just collapsed into my arms, sobbing these terrible, gut-wrenching sobs. Those bastards had really done a number on him.

I took him into the flat, tried to calm him down. He couldn't even speak.

I remembered what it had been like for me when my mother found me in bed with that bloke. She'd screamed at me, hit me, smashed my face in with the iron. Well, of course I'd told Mark none of this. How could I, just when he'd discovered he was gay? Just when he'd admitted it to himself?

I drove him to the hospital, and they took care of his nose as best they could. He discharged himself and we went back to the flat. I held him for ages and he wept like a baby on my shoulder

"I've lost everything," he said, when he'd stopped crying a bit. I had tears in my eyes, too, but they were caused more by rage than anything else. He'd opened his heart to his own family... and they'd done this to him. It was sickening.

He poured it all out, how his brother had tried to beat the shit out of him. He'd pretty much succeeded as far as I could see.

When he'd told me everything, I said, "Do you want me to go round there?"

He looked at me, clearly shocked by that idea. "How would that help?" he asked.

I didn't know how it would help; it just seemed the right thing to do. It was unfair that Mark was having to cope with all this on his own. We were in this together, after all.

For about two hours we sat there while he told me about his mum and dad, his brother and sister, how they'd always been such a close family, and now it was all wrecked. I said that nothing had been broken that couldn't be fixed, but I knew he didn't believe me. As far as he was concerned, all ties with his family had been cut forever, just because he happened to fancy boys instead of girls.

But I was hardly a shining example that things would work out in the end, was I? I hadn't spoken to my mum for almost two years. My dad knew where I lived and phoned occasionally, since he still didn't know I was gay, but we'd never been buddy-buddy, not even when I still lived at home.

It was different with Mark, though. He loved his family, he got on with them. Now they thought he was the scum of the earth.

Needless to say, he stayed at my place that night. We didn't have sex; I just held him.

He wouldn't let go.

Because at that moment, I was all he had left.

# *Mark*

SO THAT WAS it. I was out. And it was the worst thing I could possibly have done. My family despised me, Nick wanted to kill me. The only person I had left was Andrew, and even now I had mixed feelings about him. Don't get me wrong, I still knew I was gay, it was just that if it hadn't been for Andrew... maybe I'd still be in denial. But was that really a good thing, at the end of the day? Surely it was better that I be upfront about my sexuality, rather than...

Oh, who knows? If you think about it long enough it'll fry your brain. But I had no choice *but* to think about it. Before, I'd been torn between my family and my gay lover, but I'd made the choice to come out and thus face the consequences. Basically, I'd chosen my boyfriend over my family, although the bottom line was that there shouldn't have had to be a choice. Ever heard of unconditional love? Well, it seemed my family hadn't.

The following morning my face ached like hell. I thought of what had happened the day before, the moment my brother's fists had crashed into my jaw and nose. But it was the emotional pain that I felt much more than the physical. And those words. *You filthy little fucker. Get up, you filthy poof. Take your fucking medicine.*

God, how they cut me.

Thank God for Andrew and his flat. If it wasn't for that I'd have nowhere else to go. He was great... but I still couldn't believe how quickly my life had come crashing down around me.

Just 'cos I was gay.

"You okay?" he said when I woke up. He stroked my face and kissed me on the cheek.

"No," I told him. "I don't think I'll ever be okay again."

"You will," he said, and you know what? I believed him. I'm sure he was right. Eventually, things would settle down.

But 'eventually' wasn't good enough for me. I wanted things to be fine now.

If only I'd listened to Amy! She was right, had always been right. I should have just shut up about it, lived my life and got on with it. But no, I had to be clever, didn't I? Thinking I could handle it, that my family wouldn't go *that* berserk.

"What are you going to do today?" Andrew asked softly, his hand resting on my thigh.

I shrugged. "Stay here. In bed, with you. It's the only place I'm wanted," I added sadly.

He kissed me, gently on the lips, and I could feel his erection against mine and I knew then that I'd done the right thing. I was gay. People had to deal with it.

And that was that.

"You can't just give up, Mark," he told me. "What about your band? Your friends?"

*My friends.* I hadn't thought about that, hadn't thought about any of it. What about Lyar? What would the lads say when they found out about me? And I knew they would find out about me. Nick was bound to tell them; probably couldn't wait.

I started to cry. "Oh, shit, Andrew, what am I going to do?"

"You're going to live with it."

I was stunned. "That's it? That's your great advice?"

He shrugged, and then kissed me again. Beneath the covers he was still hard; though I wasn't. I felt cold and alone. It was like Andrew was throwing me to the wolves.

"You're gay," he said, in this weird businesslike voice. "If they can't deal with it, that's their problem."

"And mine."

He shook his head. "Don't say that. It's not your problem. Besides, you've still got me."

He fondled my balls, but I pushed his hand away. "Not now," I said. "I can't do it. I can't face the world." Then there was this pause that seemed to last a lifetime, before I said, "Maybe I should just move away, you know. Start a new life somewhere else." I looked at him, hope in my eyes. "We could go together."

He paused. I could tell he wanted to agree, but finally he shook his head. "What would that solve, Mark? Nothing. You can't run away from it. I mean, okay, your family are in shock right now. But maybe they'll come round to it. Maybe they'll settle down."

I could only sigh. "You don't know my family."

"Listen. People are always afraid of things they don't understand. And homosexuality is one of those things."

I started to cry again.

"Shh," said Andrew, rubbing my shoulder. "Why don't you get dressed and go round Chris's?"

I shook with the thought of that. "I can't," I said. "I can't."

"Maybe they'll be okay about it. Maybe they won't react as badly as everyone else."

*Yeah, right*, I thought, remembering the time Nick had suggested we all go to Medusa's after scoring the gig at Forbidden, what they'd said about gays.

"You'll never know if you don't go round there," Andrew said. His voice was soothing and lulling. I knew he was right. Besides, I'm sure I'd faced the worst of it.

But oh, what if it went wrong? What if I lost my band as well as my family?

The thought was too much.

But if I didn't try, I'd never know.

"I can't," I said again, frantically this time. "I can't, I can't."

"You must," said Andrew, and now he seemed suddenly older than me, older than anyone, like some great and mighty professor who knew everything.

And I knew, again, that he was right. I'd come this far, and it was surely only a matter of time before Chris, Jim and Jason knew about me. That was if they didn't know already.

"You're right," I said, and he just smiled at me.

I got out of bed, got dressed and set off. Andrew paid for my taxi and I arrived at Chris's twenty minutes later. The taxi driver was grinning at me through the rear view mirror.

"Got into a bit o' trouble last night, did ya?" he said, referring to my injured face.

I just smiled back at him. "You should've seen the other bloke," I said, feeling better already. I'd come to a decision. It was time to get on with things. Life goes on, after all, and it was time to start looking for the silver linings. There were a *few* good things about the horrible situation. Firstly, Andrew had his own flat and he loved me, so I wouldn't be homeless or alone. Secondly, even though the reaction at home had been nothing short of catastrophic, at least they *knew* now, at least there would be no more hiding, no more sneaking around.

There was still the band, though. Yet another dangerous hurdle to overcome.

Although I'd done it once, coming out, I mean, the second time was no easier. I was shaking as I mounted the steps. Everyone was already there, I could hear the music coming through the door, and I took a deep breath, and knocked.

Chris answered, his expression heavy with anger when he saw who it was. "Where were you yesterday?" he said and I was thinking, *Shit shit shit shit shit shit shit...*

But his anger turned into a frown of concern when he saw my bruises. "What happened?" he asked.

*They didn't know.*

"Mugged," I said quickly. "They just got me from behind." I was proud of my inventiveness and couldn't help but find the irony in that last sentence perversely amusing.

"Christ, Mark, they got you good, didn't they?" said Chris. "Come in, come in." He ushered me inside and when Jason and Jim saw me they were just as shocked. This wonderful sensation of relief filled me. There was hope in the world after all.

"We wondered why you didn't show up yesterday," Jason said.

"We called your house, but no one answered," Jim said.

I can do this, I told myself. I can get through this. Andrew is right, things will get better.

We jammed for a while, just old stuff, a couple of classic cover versions. Things seemed to be going well and I was planning to tell the lads about me over a couple of pints at the Lion and Eagle.

That was the plan anyway. Till Nick showed up.

# *Nick*

THE NIGHT BEFORE had been very strange. After Mark left, Anita and Amy went into the kitchen to make some tea while Mum, Dad, Tim and me stayed in the living room. We didn't speak for a while – nobody knew what to say. I was pleased Mark had gone, though. I'm sure I would've ended up killing the dirty little shit otherwise.

Mum and Dad were devastated. Mum kept crying, Dad comforting her. He seemed so old, whereas before he'd seemed so much younger than his years. He couldn't react to it. I'm not sure if it had even sunk in.

But those cold words kept echoing through my brain. *I never want to see that filthy bastard again.*

Did he mean it? I'm not sure if I wanted to see my younger brother again, but his own father?

Course, I could understand why he'd said it. My dad's a man's man, see, one of the old school. Imagine the shame of having a queer son for someone like that? How could he ever hold his head up in the local again, with everyone knowing that?

Tim tried to be sympathetic towards us all, with his "Homosexuality is nothing to be ashamed of these days" lecture. Tim *would* say that. I'd always suspected him of being a closet bender, actually. I reckon he's the type to hang around public toilets where homeless lads rent their arses to queers for a few quid.

But Mark wasn't like that. Sure, he'd always been a bit of a wimp, but he wasn't the poofy type, didn't prance around in women's underwear or anything.

So why? What had happened to change him?

I thought I knew the answer. I figured he'd been brainwashed by some dirty homo who liked the look of him, and had convinced Mark that being gay was good and right and decent. Mark's always been the stupid type, easily-led and all that. So this theory was possible.

When Anita and Amy came back with the tea, I left without a word and just walked for ages, thinking.

What a year! First all that shit happened with me and Anita, then Saffron divorced me, I was about to become a dad...

...and my brother has decided he's gay.

Well, the stuff with Anita and Saffron was bad enough for Mum and Dad to take, but at least my love life, a mess though it may have been, was focused on women. At least I wasn't getting my leg over with another fella...

Christ, the thought of it made me heave.

I mean, had he actually done it? Bent over and taken it up the...

It was too disgusting a vision to finish.

I had a beer in the Lion and Eagle, sat at a table on my own. I hated Mark so much. I wanted to kill him and half-wished Amy hadn't interfered when I'd been beating him up. How selfish he was! Look what he'd done to our family, smashed it to pieces with his sordid little sex life.

At about one o'clock in the morning, I went home to find only Anita there, sitting up waiting for me. Her eyes were all red and swollen, like she'd been crying. "Where is everyone?" I asked.

"The hospital," she said. "It's your Dad... "

"What happened?" I blurted, already fearing the worst.

"His angina played up. He was smashing Mark's room up and... collapsed."

Smashing Mark's room up? I was stunned. "He's all right now, though, right?" I said.

And to my great relief, Anita nodded. "Yeah. Amy rang a little while ago. Where have *you* been?" She was angry with me, I could tell. And I couldn't blame her. I should have been there, for God's sake! Not drowning my sorrows in some boozer.

I hugged her and kissed her hair.

"He just lost it," she said. "He was just sitting there with his arm around your mum and then he started screaming swear words, eff this and eff that. He tore upstairs and smashed Mark's room to pieces, all his stuff. That was when it came. The heart attack."

While she was telling me this I started crying. How I wanted to kill Mark! Shit, you've no idea. He'd done this. He'd nearly killed our dad.

I suggested we go to the hospital, but Anita decided against that idea. "There's nothing we can do," she said, and I knew she was right. I felt like I had to do something, though, something to make Mark pay.

I hardly slept a wink that night, just kept thinking about Mark, wondering where he was. Probably getting the living daylights banged out of him by some fucking lifter.

The next morning I called work and told them my dad had had a heart attack and that I had to go and be with him. It was the truth, but before that there was something else I had to deal with.

Mark. The pervert was gonna pay.

I didn't know what I was going to do to him, but it was going to involve pain, and it was going to involve a lot of it.

I banged on the door of Chris's flat. I could hear the band playing their music and this made me grin. Obviously they didn't know about Mark. Well they were bloody well going to find out now, courtesy of Yours Truly.

I banged on the door again, harder this time since the music was so loud. "Open up!" I shouted. The adrenaline was really going now. I couldn't wait to see Mark's face when I walked in.

It was Chris who opened up. Fat bastard. I'd never liked him.

"Nick," he said. "What do *you* want?"

"I came to see Mark," I said, trying to sound all pleasant, like this was just a friendly social visit.

Chris let me into the flat and I grinned horribly at Mark's fearful face. He knew what I was there to do, and I loved it that he knew. "All right, mate?" I said, all cheerful.

Then, "How's your bum? Had any good cocks up it lately?"

The room went silent, but only for a second. Jason and Jim started laughing, then Chris joined in. Clearly they thought I was joking.

"What about your mouth?" I said to Mark. "How does the average dick taste, eh? Or do you go in for all that kinky shit? With chocolate sauce smeared over your boyfriend's bollocks or something?"

The other's stopped laughing, hearing the poison in my

voice.

"Stop it, Nick," said Mark softly. He hadn't moved from behind his drums.

"What's wrong?" I continued. "Don't you want your mates to know their drummer's a fucking queer cunt?"

"What?" said Chris.

"He's bullshitting," said Jason. "Mark ain't... gay?"

"Oh no?" I said. "You wanna tell 'em, Marky boy? Or should that be Mark*ina* now?"

"Mark?" said Jason uncertainly. Mark said nothing. He just sat there, looking miserable, and a tiny part of me actually felt sorry for him. But then I remembered Dad, who was, at that moment, lying in a hospital bed, hooked up to all kinds of weird machines.

"Oh shit," said Jim. "He's right, isn't he, Mark?"

My brother just nodded. He closed his eyes and I saw a tear roll down his cheek.

Chris said, "I can't believe it."

"Believe it," I told him, and the hardness in my voice scared even me. "He's a bloody bender."

And it was then that I lost it. Totally. I rushed over to him, got him by the throat and held him up against the wall. Fear glowed in his eyes. "Do you know what you've done!" I shouted. "Do you know what you've fucking *done*? Right now, our father is laying in a fucking hospital bed. He had a heart attack, see, because his youngest son is so *filthy*, so *disgusting*. Did you think about that, eh? When you were letting some bloke bugger you senseless? Did you think about us?" I started crying. "I hate you, Mark. I hate you so fucking much."

I let him go and he slid to the floor in a miserable heap, sobbing. Jason, Chris and Jim were standing there with their mouths open, stunned into silence. That was pretty much the standard reaction.

I pushed past them, out of the flat and down into the cold streets below.

I walked, thinking, There has to be a way to make him straight, there *has* to be. I knew my brother, and he was no poof. All right, something or someone had made him see differently, or maybe this was a phase of some kind. Nevertheless, I was determined to make my brother the way he'd been before. I mean, how could he be gay, when Grace had told me he'd given her the best sex of her life the night they met? He fancied women, I knew he did, I only had to show him that...

And then I came up with the idea.

# Chris

I DON'T THINK any of us believed it, not at first. Not even when Nick was trying to strangle Mark. Even after Nick left, we just stood there, staring at Mark. It was so unbelievable, to imagine that Mark was gay. He was one of the lads, just like us. It didn't compute. It didn't add up.

"Mark?" I said, stepping forward. He didn't move. He was weeping, and I couldn't really blame him.

Jason and Jim were standing deadly still.

"Is it true?" I asked. "Are you gay?"

He looked up now, and I realised then that he hadn't been mugged at all, that it was obviously Nick who'd smashed his face in.

"Yes," said Mark. "Yes, I'm gay." He was coming to life now, getting really angry. "Or do you want to use one of those other words, eh? Queer? Shirt-lifter? Poofter? Bender? Go on, take your fucking pick!"

"It's true!" shouted Jason, almost gleefully. "He's a bloody poof."

Jim said, "Oh, that is *sick*!" And then awkwardly, "I mean... shit, sorry... sorry, Mark."

I was silent, for once. I felt weirdly torn in half. One half felt that we should be sticking by Mark, no matter what his sexual preference was. But the other half was disgusted by the whole thing. I'd never understood homosexuality; I still don't. Why shag a bloke when there're so many gorgeous birds out there practically begging for it?

And the idea that Mark could be one of *them*... Christ, it was unreal.

He got to his feet and was suddenly full of all this hatred, all this hostility. "So, you want to have a pop at me?" he snapped. "Kick the crap out of me? Go on, go ahead. Here I am, boys. Go mad, eh?"

None of us knew what to say to that.

"Mark, look... " I began, but I couldn't finish. What was I supposed to say to him? *It doesn't matter, Mark? Never mind that you're gay?*

I should've said that, shouldn't I?

I should've... but I didn't. Because it *did* matter that he was gay. It shouldn't have mattered... but it did. I couldn't cope with the fact, and you can chuck all the names in the world at me – bigot, homophobe, prejudice, arsehole – it won't change a thing.

I looked at Mark and saw him in a different light. Gone was the fun-loving drummer who wanted our band to be successful so badly he could taste it. All he was to me now was a pansy, a sissy... a queer. He could see that just by looking into my eyes. He saw what I thought of him, of his kind.

He saw... and then he left.

## *Mark*

I WANTED TO be dead. I wanted it so much I almost walked out into the road, in front of a bus. I was sure death would be easier to face than life had been – my life, anyway. Why did it have to be so cruel? Why did there have to be such things as sexuality, love and desires? Why did there have to be such difficult choices to make?

I walked for a long time before deciding on any particular destination. I couldn't go home. I couldn't go to Chris's. I couldn't go to the hospital to see my father. I didn't want to go to Andrew's. In a way, I blamed him for all this. Why couldn't he have just left me to make my own decision? Why had he bullied me into coming out? Why had he...

But I was just using him for a scapegoat. Like I told you at the beginning, *I* made the decision to come out. No one made it for me. Not my friends, my family, or my boyfriend.

Or girlfriend.

Grace didn't know about me yet, unless Nick had told her...

But then I realised. Anita was Grace's sister. Anita had been there when I came out. Anita knew.

I felt sick with dread.

Not Grace, too. I didn't want to lose Grace as a friend. Okay, so we could never be anything more than that, but... oh, not Grace...

I ran to the nearest bus stop and went straight to her flat. All these thoughts of hope were rushing through my head. Maybe Anita hadn't told her. Maybe she thought it was up to me to break the news. Maybe... maybe...

But there was no more time for maybes.

I knocked on the door with a barely steady hand. Half of me prayed she was in.

The other half hoped she was not.

# *Grace*

I WAS ASLEEP when he came round. It was my day off, actually, and I'd taken a couple of Nytol, just to help me sleep. The only thing was, they worked too well and I'd be out of it till around one the next day. So you can imagine I was pretty narked when I had to get up to answer the door.

You're probably wondering why I didn't just stay in bed. Well, believe me I wanted to, but something told me that I had to answer, that it was someone important. And as it turned out, that feeling was pretty accurate.

When I first saw it was Mark, I thought, *Shit, look at the state of me*. I was only wearing a tatty old T-shirt.

But then I looked more clearly at him, his face all punched in and bruised, his eyes all red and tearful, and there was this great red mark around his throat.

"Mark, what happened?" I cried, flinging my arms around him. My first thought was that he'd been mugged and that made me feel sick because I already knew his dad was in hospital after suffering a heart attack. Anita had called the night before to tell me she was staying at Nick's, but she was dead evasive, which I have to say made me a bit suspicious.

"You don't know yet, do you?" he said as we sat down on our sofa, the same sofa we'd both smoked dope on the night we met.

"Yes," I told him. "I do know. Anita called."

"Oh," was all he said. He looked really ashamed of himself, really guilty, like it was his fault his dad was in hospital and then I started to wonder if the state of his face meant that he'd tried to do himself in.

"It wasn't your fault, Mark," I told him, putting a hand on his knee.

"No?" He gave me this look then, kind of like an abandoned puppy. I felt so sorry for him.

"Of course it wasn't, Mark."

He shook his head. "I shouldn't have told him. I shouldn't

have told him."

I frowned and said, "Told him what? What are you talking about?" and now when he looked at me there was a new light in his eyes; a light called fear. I grew cold. "Mark?" I said. "What are you on about? What shouldn't you have told your Dad?"

"About me being gay," he said.

It was like a slap in the gob. My first reaction was to laugh. "You? You're... gay?" Then I frowned. I looked into his eyes and I knew he wasn't joking. "You can't be," I said. "That night we... we... you made love to me, Mark. I'm a woman, you're a man. You can't be gay." I must have sounded like a blabbering idiot, but I couldn't get my head round what he was saying.

"I'm sorry, Grace," he said. "I was kidding myself. Hiding from the truth."

"You're not gay, Mark," I said. I wasn't having it. He could not be gay. My boyfriend could not be gay. And then it dawned on me. I knew who must have been responsible. "It's Andrew, isn't it, Mark? He's convinced you you're gay somehow. Shit, I should've known he was up to no good when he said he fancied you."

I'd known Andrew for a while, ever since me and a couple of mates had discovered Medusa's a couple of years back. He was a good bloke, nice-looking, friendly. We'd had a laugh together a few times, just at the bar, you know. Then one night he'd let slip that he fancied Mark and there was this look about him that seemed to say *I'm gonna get him. Oh yes I am. Just you wait and see.*

"It's Andrew, isn't it?" I repeated and Mark nodded.

"Yes." And then came the death blow: "We've been seeing each other... for a while."

His answer floored me. I couldn't find any words for a full minute. "Christ, no wonder your old man's where he is." That was an unfair thing to say, and I knew it, but you have to understand how hurt I was. I'd never been so hurt. It was awful, this deep, raw wound inside me. So that was why our relationship had grown so cold, 'cos he and Andrew had been at it behind my back.

I don't think you can actually know how awful it is to discover your boyfriend has been cheating on you with another man unless it's actually happened to you. I mean, bad enough if your bloke's been unfaithful, but for him to be unfaithful *and* gay? It was a double assault!

Now, let me make it quite clear that I have ABSOLUTELY NOTHING against gays. Firstly, I think it's cool to be gay, secondly gay men are the loveliest blokes in the world, and thirdly this *is* the nineties.

But it's quite a different matter when your boyfriend has been... well, lying to you. I mean, that was the bottom line, wasn't it? He'd been lying to me. What other words were there for it?

While he'd been making love to me, had he been imagining I was a man, that I was Andrew...?

*Oh, God.*

That did it. I slapped him hard across the face. He didn't say or do anything. It was like he knew he deserved it, like he'd been expecting it.

I started to cry. "How could you?" I blurted. "I thought you loved me, Mark."

"I *do* love you!" he said, tears in his eyes as well. "I just didn't realise I was gay at the time."

"Don't be so stupid!" I screamed at him. "You just didn't realise? When you were humping me in the bedroom you *didn't realise?*"

Yeah, I know it sounds crude, but I was upset.

"Grace, please... " he said. He put an arm on my shoulder and I shook him off.

"Don't touch me," I told him. "Get out, Mark. Don't call me. Don't come round here."

"No, Grace, we can still be friends," he said, all desperate and frantic. "Please, I've lost everything. My family, my band. I don't want to lose you, too. You're my best friend. Grace, please." He was really sobbing now, his body shaking.

But I couldn't forgive him; I couldn't. I was too deeply hurt.

"You should've thought about that before," I hissed.

"I didn't think you minded gays," he said.

I glared at him. "I don't care if you're gay or straight, Mark. That isn't an issue. If you'd've told me right from the beginning, I wouldn't have given a shit. It's that you *lied* to me."

"But I didn't lie – "

"Shut up!" I screamed, slapping him again.

"Grace... "

"Get out, Mark. Get out!"

And he went.

# *Amy*

I'D ONLY POPPED home to feed the cat. I wasn't expecting to find Mark there on the sofa. I'd given everyone a key to the house when I'd first moved in, in case of emergencies.

I said, "What are you doing here?" There was anger in my voice, and with good cause. If you'd seen my dad, lying there in that hospital bed, believe me, you'd understand.

He just looked at me. His face was all broken and bruised and I felt so sorry for him... but so pissed off at the same time. This was HIS FAULT, after all, not because he was gay, but because he'd told the family. I mean, how stupid was he? Knowing our family and everything. The original traditionalists. Seriously, our dad accept that his youngest is gay? It was laughable to imagine anything less than what had happened.

And I told him not to say anything. I made him promise me for God's sake!

And he told anyway.

When I first discovered him in bed with that bloke, to tell the honest truth I wasn't all that surprised. He wasn't effeminate or anything, Mark, I mean, he just had this... I don't know, gay quality to him. It's something I can't quite put my finger on, you know?

Not that I minded, of course. To be gay in the nineties... well, it's pretty fashionable, isn't it? If you're open-minded, that is. But for people from my parents' generation – forget it. All they see is dirty, filthy perverts, and there's no getting away from that.

But it seemed Mark had seen things differently, had thought he could get away with it. What a joke.

Now Dad was in hospital, Mum was a mess, Nick wanted to kill Mark. And Mark himself? Well, he was far from fine.

"I had to see you," he told me, in this pitiful squeak of a voice.

"Why?" I snapped. I went into the kitchen where Sox, my little tabby cat, was asleep by the cupboard where we kept the cat food. She perked up as soon as she saw me and started meowing at the top of her tiny lungs. I smiled and fed her and just a little part of the ice in me melted. Mark had followed me into the kitchen and he stood in the doorway, leaning against the frame as if he didn't even have the strength to hold himself up. He looked truly exhausted.

"Don't expect me to feel sorry for you, Mark," I said crossly, though it was getting harder and harder to be angry when he looked so pathetic and used up. "I warned you this would happen, if you told. Why did you have to do it?"

He said, "I just... I don't know. I suppose I thought... it would be all right. Somehow."

I laughed, incredulously. "Mark, do you know what you've done to this family?"

He nodded weakly.

"I mean, do you have any idea the state we're all in. Dad nearly died. Mum's in a state of shock. Nick's out for your blood."

"And what about you?" he asked.

The question threw me slightly. "Me?" I said. "I don't know what to think. You promised me you wouldn't tell. I said I didn't mind that you were gay, and I don't. But you *knew* Mum and Dad would. I mean, it doesn't take a genius to work out what they'd do. I just can't figure it out. *Why did you tell them?*"

"I don't know!" he screamed. "I don't know!"

"To ease your conscience, was it?" I went on relentlessly. "To make you feel better? Well, I tell you something, mate, feeling better is something that this family may never do again. You and your little secret has blown us eight ways from Sunday!"

"Please, Amy," he begged, taking a trembly step towards me. "Please don't desert me, too. I'll have nothing left."

"What about your boyfriend?"

"I don't want to have to choose, Amy. I want my family as well as Andrew."

*Andrew*, I thought. *So that's his name.*

"You've already chosen," I told him. "You chose to tell, now you have to face the consequences."

"I don't want to."

"Tough." How bitter I sounded. How hateful. But I

couldn't control my rage. I said, "If it had been anything else, Mark. If you'd've been a junkie, or an alcoholic, or in trouble with the police, I'm sure they would've been able to accept it. But not this. This is the absolute limit."

"It shouldn't have to be," he said.

"No," I agreed. "It shouldn't have to be. But it is. And what gets me, is that you knew what they'd do. You're twenty, for crying out loud. Not some dumb twelve-year-old."

"I know. I'm sorry."

"It's too late for sorry. Dad said he never wants to see you again, and Mum'll agree with that, you know what she's like. And if it was up to Nick he'd have you hung, drawn and quartered."

The pain on my little brother's face broke my heart. "Amy, please... " he trailed, unable to finish the sentence. "Don't do this." He stared at the floor. Tear drops spattered on the linoleum.

"Oh, Mark," I sighed, moving towards him and wrapping my arms around his shivering body. "Oh, Mark, what have you done, eh? What have you done?"

# Nick

I WAS ONLY going to hire the one, but I thought if there were two it'd make things easier on Mark. What am I talking about, you ask? Ah ha. You'll find out soon enough.

I wasn't giving up, see. Bottom line: Mark was straight. I *knew* he was straight. I didn't know what had happened to him to make him gay, but it wasn't permanent. It couldn't be. And with a little help from his friends, and his older brother, he'd be cured.

It took me a while to sort out the details of the plan, but once I'd done that, I was away. I couldn't do it alone, though, so at about three I went round Chris's again, hoping that Mark wouldn't be there. I was pretty sure he wouldn't be, though, not after *my* little intervention.

Fortunately, it turned out that Jim, Jason and Chris were all up for the idea. They agreed with me that Mark was really straight and they all thought the plan would help him to see this.

Besides, they had an important gig on Saturday and they needed him with them because the talent scout would be there. So it was all ready. I'd hired the... props, let's call them for now, Chris had agreed we could use his flat.

Now all we needed... was Mark.

# Grace

I MISSED HIM already. He'd only been gone a few hours, and already I wanted him back. The boyfriend thing wasn't as much of an issue as I thought. I mean, we hadn't known each other long enough for things to get serious. Sure, we'd had sex, but it was really only on a casual basis, I suppose.

The thing was, though, we'd been really good friends, despite all that relationship junk. He'd helped me through all the stuff with Anita, and to top it all we got on really well.

Once I'd got over the fact that he was gay, I started to calm down a bit. Mark hadn't really betrayed me – well, not much. And certainly not out of malice. He must have been so confused, I couldn't *begin* to imagine. But it really was a stupid thing to do, wasn't it, telling his parents?

Don't get me wrong, Maeve and Bill are lovely people, they're just old-fashioned and set in their ways. You would've thought that Mark, their own son, would've had the sense to keep his gob shut, wouldn't you?

Hm. Well, he may have been a brilliant drummer, but he obviously lacked common sense.

I couldn't bear the way I'd spoken to him, with his face all mangled up. I sat there for a long time after he left, still in my tatty old T-shirt. Those words kept going over and over in my head, so pitiful, so broken. *No Grace, we can still be friends. Please, I've lost everything.*

Lost everything. Imagine the horror of that, to have your family turn so fully, so violently against you. It would be like drowning in a tidal wave, to feel the entire force of their hatred and anger and disgust crushing you flat.

*You're my best friend.* That's what he'd told me. And it was true. We were best friends.

And right then, in that tiny, minuscule split second, I knew I had to forgive him. Because if I didn't, I'd be just as bad as those other bastards; as bad as Nick and Chris and every other stupid, prejudiced, ignorant moron in the world.

*We can still be friends, Grace.*

Yeah, Mark, I thought, getting to my feet. We can still be friends.

Because if there's to be any hope of love anywhere, then there has to be the chance to try again.

But where? Where was I supposed to begin my search? After the day Mark had had, he could be anywhere. He could've even tried to...

No. I was going to be positive about this.

The first place was obvious – his house. I banged on the door for ages, but nobody answered. It made sense. They were probably all at the hospital.

The next nearest place was Chris's flat. It was a long shot, but even if Mark wasn't there, then surely the others had to be and maybe – just maybe – they could give me some clue as to his whereabouts.

I knocked for ages, rang the doorbell, and just as I was about to give up, Chris answered. He was red in the face, as if embarrassed, and wearing just a white bath robe. He looked pretty pissed off to see me, only opening the door a crack. "Oh, it's you," he said. "What?"

"Is Mark there?"

"Mark?" said Chris, as if he had no idea who I was talking about.

"Yeah, Mark. Is he there?"

"No," said Chris quickly. "No, he's not here."

In the background I thought I heard the sounds of a woman giggling and then it hit me that that was why Chris was so eager to get rid of me. I must have interrupted him giving that bimbo Gloria a seeing to.

"Why aren't you rehearsing?" I said.

He just shrugged. "We're allowed to take some time off, you know. Now, was there anything else?"

"Do you know where Mark might be?"

He shrugged, then with a disgusting smirk said, "Try the YMCA. See you, Grace." And he shut the door on me.

Pig.

My next stop was Medusa's, where Andrew worked. Not surprisingly, the place was closed, but I thought I'd try my luck anyway. I banged on the door and called, "Hellooo! Anyone there! It's an emergency!"

It took a while, but somebody opened at last, a young black bloke in a long leather coat whom I'd never laid eyes on before. "What's the emergency?" he said.

"Thank God!" I cried, so relieved I could have kissed him. "Listen, I need to speak to a bloke called Andrew. He works here and – "

"Yeah, yeah, I know Andrew," the bloke interrupted. "His shift doesn't start till nine, though."

My heart fell.

"I could give you his address, though." The bloke squinted at me, as if suspicious. "You a friend of his, then?"

"I'm his sister," I told him, improvising.

"Sister? He's never mentioned anything about a sister before."

"He doesn't know about me. I'm... adopted." I thought, *Christ, what's this turning into?*

"Adopted?"

"That's right. I found out about a month ago. I'm down from, uh, Bristol."

"Mm," he said but I couldn't tell if he was convinced.

"I'd really appreciate it," I added.

And then after another pause, the bloke said, "Well, okay then. Wait here a second I'll get you his address."

"Thank you," I told him. "I'm very grateful."

He gave a nod and vanished back inside the club, returning a few minutes later with a hastily scribbled address. "You sure you're his sister?" he said, handing it to me.

I grinned. "Very sure. Listen, I have to go. Thanks for your help." And then I was off.

I didn't have enough money for a taxi, so I got the bus. Andrew's flat was quite nearby, so it didn't take me long.

I just prayed he'd be in. I had this weird hot feeling at the bottom of my heart that I had to find Mark, that something horrible was going to happen to him if I didn't. Call it female intuition, or a psychic premonition if you like, whatever. The important thing is that I *knew.*

I knocked on the door of the flat. Mark had to be there.

Where else *could* he be?

Andrew opened wearing just boxer shorts and – embarrassingly – I thought: *What a shame he's gay.*

"Grace?" he said, clearly shocked to see me. "How did you – "

I interrupted. "Where's Mark?"

"Mark? I don't know. I haven't seen him." Andrew suddenly looked very worried. "Has something happened to him? It's that arsehole brother of his, isn't it?"

"Nick?" I said, my heart racing. I shook my head. "Look, Andrew, I don't know. I've been looking all over for Mark."

"Why?"

I bowed my head, ashamed of myself, remembering the way I'd spoken to him. "We had a row."

"He's told you then?"

"Yes. I kicked him out, Andrew. I turned him away when he needed me. But... I've calmed down now. I want to say I'm sorry, that we can still be friends."

"And now you can't find him?"

"No."

"You have no idea where he is?"

"No."

"How did you get my address?"

"I asked some bloke at Medusa's. I said I was your adopted sister."

Andrew looked stunned.

"But never mind about that," I said. "We've got to find Mark."

"Why?"

I shook my head. "I'm not sure, Andrew. I've... I've just got this really bad feeling."

# Mark

I HAD TO go to the hospital. Dumb idea? Maybe, but over the past two days I'd had quite a few of those. So I figured one more wouldn't make much difference.

I stayed at Amy's for a while, talking things out. I told her how terrible it had all been for me, not just what had taken place over the last couple of days, but also making the discovery, accepting the fact that I was definitely, one-hundred percent homosexual.

She cried. I cried. We hugged. And then I suggested I go to the hospital, try and make it up with Dad.

Well, of course, you can imagine the reaction that got.

"Haven't you learnt anything?" she screeched, and there we were, right back at the beginning. "No, Mark," she went on. "I forbid you to go. What if Dad has another attack, eh? He was lucky before. What if this time he dies? How are you going to be able to live with that? You're not going, Mark."

I sighed. "I have to. Will you drive me?"

She just looked at me, slack-jawed. "You're not serious?"

"Very. If you don't drive me, I'll get the bus. I'll walk if I have to."

She put her head in her hands. "Mark, please. Don't go. Don't go. I'm begging you."

"I have to."

"No, you – "

"I'm going, Amy. You can't stop me." I got up to leave.

"Wait!" she said. She grabbed my arm. There was a long pause, and she finally said, "All right, I'll drive you. But let me go in first, okay? See how the land lies."

I sighed. "Okay."

We didn't speak during the journey. Amy had borrowed Tim's car, and as we pulled into the car park the phone rang. It was Nick, wanting to know where I was. Amy told him, and I could hear his foul-mouthed words of protest as clearly as if it was I that held the phone.

She just hung up on him. "Come on," she told me. "Let's get this over with."

We headed straight up to the ward Dad was on and I waited outside. "I'll be back in a few minutes, okay?" Amy said. "*Don't* come in before I get back, right?"

I nodded solemnly. The dreadful hospital smell filled my head with visions of death and funerals. I'd always hated hospitals.

Amy returned a few minutes later. "He's sleeping," she said. "And Mum doesn't want you anywhere near him."

God, how those words hurt.

"But – " I began.

"Leave it, Mark," said Amy. "Leave it."

And I knew I had no choice. I nodded sadly.

"I'll drive you back," she said.

"No," I told her. "You go sit with Mum. I'll be all right."

"Are you sure?"

"I'm sure."

She kissed me quickly on the cheek and then turned, going back into the ward. I was so close to crying I couldn't stand it. But I wouldn't break down. Not there.

The car park was freezing cold and my face hurt with all the bruises, but very slowly I started to walk towards the bus stop.

Then behind me, Nick's voice called my name.

I spun, as if being attacked. And there was my brother, leaning against Chris's van.

*Chris's van?*

I was shocked. Nick started to walk towards me, and that was enough for me. I legged it. He wasn't going to give up until I was dead, was he?

But of course, Nick, with all his athletic prowess, easily caught up with me. He put a heavy hand on my shoulder, stopping me dead in my tracks. "Nick, please," I begged. "Please, don't do it. I can't help the way I am, I can't – "

"Hey, hey, it's all right," he said softly. "I came to apologise to you. I'm sorry, Mark. Christ, what have I done to you, eh?"

I was speechless. Nick? *Apologising?*

I said, "What's with the van?"

He looked over his shoulder. "Oh, yeah. Right. Erm... my car broke down. I had to get here, so I asked Chris. That's where I called Amy from, Chris's. When she told me you were here, I came right over. Did you see Dad?"

I shook my head. "No. He didn't want to know."

Nick smiled, a warm, brotherly smile. It was the old Nick. He said, "Give it time, mate. The old man'll come to his senses soon. I have."

"Really?" I said, half of me believing, the other half not so sure.

"Really. Now come on. Let's go home."

I grinned. "Thanks, Nick."

"Hey," he said, as we started to walk, "what are big brothers for, eh?"

# Nick

MY LITTLE BROTHER'S so stupid. I'd already kicked the shit out of him twice, but here he still was, following me to the van, like I'd forgiven him, like I'd accepted he was a bender.

I don't *think* so.

But even though he was trusting me, I was still determined to go through with the plan. I was helping him, that's all, curing him. Okay, it might not have seemed that way at the time, but believe me, it was for his own good.

We climbed into the van and I pulled away, turning on the radio as we went. I turned it up to its full volume, so that we wouldn't be able to speak. It was for the best. I didn't want Mark to start blabbing on about how great it was that I'd accepted his gayness. I couldn't've handled that.

We arrived at Chris's flat, the place where we'd decided to execute the plan.

"Why are we here?" asked Mark. "I thought we were going home."

"We'll get a bus the rest of the way," I said, delivering my lines perfectly. "I promised Chris I'd drop the van off at about now."

"Have they said anything to you?" he said. "About me being in the band?"

"No," I lied. "Nothing."

I got out of the van, went round and opened Mark's door. He said, "I don't want to go up."

"Come on," I told him. "They'll be all right. I am, aren't I? If you can win me over, you can win anyone over."

This seemed to work. After a short pause, he got out of the van and we went up together. Adrenaline was rushing through me as we knocked on the door. In a couple of seconds, the final phase of the plan would be put into action. I just hoped the others were ready.

Mark said, "Are you sure they're – "

But he didn't have a chance to finish. The door was flung open and Jason and Jim grabbed him and yanked him in. I followed slowly, hating myself for feeling nervous.

Mark was clearly shocked – who wouldn't be? "What's going on?" he spluttered, and I thought, *Fucking little wimp.*

Out loud I said, "This is for you own good, Mark. We're going to make you better."

Chris was standing by the bedroom door, just as we'd discussed.

"It's all right, Mark," he said. "We're going to cure you."

And Jason and Jim shoved him inside before Chris locked the door. You're probably wondering why we'd done this, locked my little brother in an empty room. Well, it wasn't empty. Remember earlier, when I said I thought I'd hire two instead of one? I'd been talking about prostitutes, see? Hookers, whores, slags. The real slutty kind, too, who'd do *anything*. Back-door sex, hand-relief, doggy style... you name it. Me and the other lads had all chipped in and bunged the slappers two-hundred quid, with express instructions to give Mark what he wanted. 'Course we'd had a taste as well, but it *was* our money, after all.

Well, we'd done as much as we could for Mark. He was in there with two big-titted babes who'd open their legs as wide as he wanted and let him do what blokes do best. Now we just had to wait for the action to begin and pretty soon, Mark Holly would be a poofter no more.

# *Jason*

IT WAS WRONG. I knew it was wrong; had known all along, in fact. No, not Mark being gay, I don't mean that. I mean what we were trying to do to him, what Nick was trying to do to him. Lock him in a room with a couple of hookers for him to bang till he realised being queer was the filthiest thing in the world.

Wrong. Nick's plan was the filthiest thing in the world.

"Go on!" Nick was shouting through the door. "Go for your life, mate! They're all for you! They'll do anything you want, mate!"

How perverse it all was. I felt sick and I knew I shouldn't have gone along with it; I should've stopped it from happening. But I was a wimp, a coward. I thought if I said something, they might think I was gay an' all. And I didn't want to cross that line.

But now, with Mark in there with those prozzies... shit, it was all I could do not to throw up with self-loathing.

"Go on, Mark!" Chris joined in. "Give 'em what for!"

I knew for a fact that Chris and Nick had 'given 'em what for', too. "Well," they'd said. "While we're paying and all that."

They'd asked me if I wanted a piece of the action, but I'd turned them down. "I don't need to pay for sex," I said, which was true. I wasn't a bad-looking lad; I could easily find a girl-friend. And to be honest, the thought of doing it with those whores in there... yuck.

You could hear their voices coming through the door, all breathy and sexy. "Come on, Mark," said one of them. "We know you're a big boy down below. Tell us what you want, eh? Doggy-dog? Oil? We're all paid up, you know. Go nuts."

And then the second slut: "How about I give you a good sucking, eh? Or how about you let me ride while my friend sits on your face? What about that?"

I have to admit that their sleazy talk made me hard. Still, I hated myself for it.

"Go on, Mark!" Nick said joyfully. "What are you waiting

for? Forget about being bent and tuck in!"

From Mark there was no response and it was at this point that I decided to excuse myself. "I need some fresh air," I said.

"You'll miss all the fun," Chris said, but he kept his ear against the door, an inane grin on his fat red face.

I shrugged. "I'll get over it," I said sarcastically.

I left the flat and went downstairs into the street, leaning against the wall and trying to forget about what was happening upstairs. I couldn't. Poor Mark. He was being treated like a Jew in Nazi Germany. This was the nineties, for fuck's sake!

I had to help Mark. If I didn't, who would? If he didn't make it with those prozzies, what would Nick do to him then? He'd kill him!

My first thought was to call the police. But no. Stupid idea. I didn't want to involve the law. But who else? Mark's family wouldn't give a shit. So the only other person was... Grace.

## Mark

I FELT LIKE a Christian being fed to the lions. The whores sat there in their tacky tart's gear, done up to the nines. And I was supposed to do it with them? Sick.

I stayed with my back to the wall while they undressed and started to masturbate. It was supposed to turn me on. Right.

I couldn't believe Nick had done this to me. I couldn't believe I'd been so stupid in believing he didn't care that I was gay.

Bastard!

"Come on," one of the sluts said, a blonde woman, sliding over to me and rubbing my leg. "Your brother's paid me, with strict instructions to give you what you want. So how about you tell me, eh? How about you tell Auntie Scarlett what you want?"

I stayed against the wall.

From outside, Nick's voice said savagely, "Do it, Mark. Do it!"

"No," I whispered, watching the prostitutes like they were creatures in a zoo.

I pressed my back up against the door as they advanced, looking like hungry vampires.

"He's not going for it," one of them called out, the one who'd called herself 'Auntie Scarlett'.

And then behind me, the door was flung violently open and I tumbled out onto the threadbare carpet. "What's wrong with you?" Nick was screeching, staring down at me. "What's fucking *wrong* with you?"

I tried to speak, but he kicked me in the head. "All right, lads," he said. "Hold him down. Get his strides off."

Oh, the shame of it. The fucking shame of it as Chris and Jim pulled off first my trousers, then my boxers. They held my legs down and Nick said to the prostitutes, "Go on. Do it. Do your work. Cure him."

"I don't think we... " one of them trailed, and I could tell she was scared. I don't blame her. Nick was like a madman.

"Do what I'm fucking paying you for!" he screamed.

The other hooker said nervously, "Look, you said he'd be up for it, he obviously isn't. This is too fucking weird, all right. Come on, Scarlett, let's go."

Nick let go of my arms and I tried to get up but Chris was too quick, pinning me down while Jim kept hold of my bare legs. I heard Nick's heavy footsteps stamping across the floor and then this loud *Smack!* like a hand connecting with a vulnerable cheek. Then there was this *Whumph!* sound. Like a sack of potatoes being dumped on the floor. All I could see was Chris's dirty ceiling, but I knew what Nick was doing. Beating the shit out of the prostitutes.

I heard the scuffle continue as the other girl tried to fend him off, but of course she was no match for him. There was another loud slapping sound and then the second woman went down. I turned my head slightly and saw them both on the floor, struggling to get up.

"Fucking lying slags!" shouted Nick. "Fucking disobedient cunts!"

I'd never seen Nick like this. So wild. So out of control.

Jim and Chris let go of me and I sat up, putting a hand over my exposed genitals.

"Calm down, Nick," said Chris.

"Take it easy, mate," said Jim.

They both tried in vain to hold him back.

The prostitutes were crawling out the door, still wearing all their gear. If the scene hadn't been so awful, I would probably have laughed.

"Get the fuck off me," hissed Nick to Chris and Jim. "A lot of fucking help you two were." And then he looked at me, and there was such rage and hate in his eyes that I actually flinched. "And you?" he spat. "You still queer, eh? Still a fucking bum bandit? You must be adopted, you sick bastard. You must be fucking adopted."

It amazed me that after everything that had happened, his words could still cut so deeply.

Chris and Jim left the flat. I couldn't believe it, even though it was Chris's flat, they still went, too scared of Nick to hang around and help me.

I'd never felt more alone in my life.

# Andrew

THE SITUATION WAS wired, like a bomb about to go off. It was kind of exciting, in a sick sort of way. Me and Grace had gone back to her flat, ringing round everywhere we could think of to find Mark. His house, Chris's house, his brother's house. No joy. It was so frustrating. And Grace wasn't helping matters much by going on about 'bad feelings'. She was putting out these really tense vibes, which made me start to worry, too.

I had no idea how Mark was feeling, how could I? When my homosexuality came out in the open – well, when my mum caught me at it – things were so different for me. For a start, I didn't have a psychotic brother out to get me; I didn't have a particularly bright future ahead of me, unlike Mark, and also I hadn't had a girlfriend.

Plus I hadn't fully come out, had I? Not really. It was only Mum who knew about me.

Mark was so much braver. What guts he had, to tell his family in one go.

Okay, it had turned out to be a pretty stupid move, but you can't have everything.

"I give up," Grace said at last. "He could be on a train to Timbuk-bloody-too by now."

"No, he won't," I said, but to be honest her words scared me a bit. I didn't want to lose Mark. I loved him. But I had the nervous feeling that love wouldn't be enough to help him out of the shit he was in.

Me and Grace just sat there for a while, not speaking, just staring at the wall, as if we were waiting for an answer to just pop out of the sky.

And then there was a knock at the door. I thought, *Mark! Thank Christ!* and I'm sure Grace did the same. We looked at each other with these great big toothy grins, eyes dancing with relief.

Yes, he's safe. He made it.

There was another knock on the door. *Bangbangbang!* Really dramatic and desperate.

"Well, what are we waiting for?" I said. I got to my feet and answered the front door.

But it wasn't Mark. At first I didn't recognise the bloke, but then I realised it was the guitar player from Lyar, the youngest. I couldn't for the life of me remember his name. But that didn't matter. I was so gutted that it hadn't been Mark and once again my head went crazy with all these images of him lying stabbed to death in some ditch.

"Jason?" said Grace, standing behind me. "What are you doing here?" Clearly she was just as shocked to see him as I was, and just as disappointed that he wasn't Mark.

The bloke's face was really red, and he was so out of breath, like he was on the run from the law or something. "It's Mark," he said, and my heart leapt in my chest.

"What's happened to him?" I asked.

Jason shook his head, catching his breath. "He's in trouble. Some really bad shit."

Grace gasped. "What? Where?"

"At Chris's. Nick's – "

"What?" I demanded, cutting him off.

"They locked him in a room with these two hookers for him to – "

"Mother*fuck*!" I cried, already knowing what they'd done to him. Shit, it was unbelievable. Just who was the real pervert, eh? Mark for being gay, or Nick for doing what he was doing?

I think you know the answer.

Grace went, "Oh... " and I thought she was going to faint.

I said, "We have to call the police."

"No!" said Jason. "We shouldn't get the police involved."

"We have to," said Grace. "What if Mark doesn't do what Nick wants him to? Nick might kill him!"

She was right. We all knew she was right, but only Grace dared to say it. Nick would kill him.

"Call the police, Grace," I said.

She moved to the phone.

"No!" said Jason. "Don't involve the police. It'll only make things worse."

"How can things possibly get any worse?" I said. "Think of Mark."

Jason looked really pained, as if he might start crying. "But I... I helped them do it," he faltered. "I'll be an accessory."

I frowned, then sighed. "You did the right thing in the end, though, mate," I told him. But I had to wonder if that really made any difference. If you did something bad, did it get cancelled out if you went back and said sorry as quickly as you could?

I said, "Call the police, Grace."

And she did.

# Mark

SO THERE YOU have it. That's my story. Not exactly a happy ending, is it? Well, that's life, I guess, and there are few happy endings nowadays, aren't there? You might even say that they're becoming an endangered species. Still, things seem to be getting back to normal now.

As it turned out, I only needed to spend one night in hospital, just for observation. I was lucky, see. Nick didn't beat me up too much before the police arrived, he spent most of the time mouthing off about how disgusting I was. But that hurt more, in a way.

He got two years for GBH. Amazingly, the prostitutes testified against him. Everyone reckons he'll be out in a few months, with good behaviour or something. But the thing is, I don't feel pleased he's locked away, just sad. Maybe if I'd kept my mouth shut, things would just be the same as they were before.

Well, no they wouldn't, would they? I'd still be miserable, living my life like some kind of spy.

Me and Andrew live together in his flat. Things are great between us, I really love him, and now I've got a whole load of new friends, some gay, some straight. But I've learnt a lot, you know. Sexuality doesn't change anything between REAL friends. When it comes down to it, it's all a matter of taste, right? Some people like coffee, others don't. Some people like Indian food, others don't. Some blokes fancy men, others don't. Simple, see?

As for my dad, well... he came out of hospital, right as ninepence. I'm wise enough to know things can never be the same again between us, but I guess I'll have to learn to live with that. We're on speaking terms again, though. But only just. Sometimes I see him in the local and he says hello and how are you. That's about it, though. Still, it's early days yet, isn't it?

My mum's coping pretty well. She's been round to see me and Andrew a few times, reckons he's a lovely lad. And she's got her new granddaughter now. Yeah, Anita had the baby. Melody, she named her, and she takes her to see Nick every fortnight.

Maybe being a dad will help Nick to grow up a bit, who knows? She's a right little ray of sunshine, though, is Melody. She really takes up Mum and Dad's time, when Anita has to work or something, which I can only see as a good thing.

Let's see, what else is there? Oh, yeah! Grace. She got married last month, to – you'll never guess – Jason. They'd only been seeing each other for a few weeks before getting hitched. Of course, I was the best man.

Lyar split up after the showdown at Chris's flat. I didn't want anything more to do with those fuckers Jim and Chris after they'd set me up like that, but I'm still mates with Jason and there's talk of us setting up our own band. I'm sure me and him were the only *real* talent in Lyar, anyway.

As for Chris and Jim, I don't know what they're up to, and I can't really say I give a shit. Wankers.

Amy's still great. She's pregnant now as well. I'm really chuffed for her. I know she and Tim have wanted a baby for ages, and it'll be nice for Melody to have a little playmate.

I'm not sure if Anita and Nick will get married. After everything that happened I think Anita's seen a side of Nick that she doesn't like. Well, there's always a chance he'll change when he gets out of prison, I guess. Who can say? Time will just have to tell.

Time's a funny thing. A year ago, I thought I was straight, now I'm gay. But that's the *real* truth. You can't escape the truth, you can't get away from it, you can't outrun it, because it will always catch up with you in the end. And that's what happened to me: truth caught up. I'm happier now, though, even after everything else, I'm happier than I've ever been. I've got a great boyfriend, great friends, and I'm no longer an outcast in my own family. Well... not much, eh?

I've learnt some hard, but valuable lessons recently, but the one that sticks in my head the most is this: before you can get anywhere with anything, you have to be honest with yourself.

At the end of the day, that's the only thing that counts.

See ya.

Send for our free catalogue to GMP Publishers Ltd,
BCM 6159, London WC1N 3XX, England

*Gay Men's Press* books can be ordered from any bookshop in the
UK, North America and Australia, and from
specialised bookshops elsewhere.

Our distributors whose addresses are given in the front pages of
this book can also supply individual customers by mail order.
Send retail price as given plus 10% for postage and packing.

*For payment by Mastercard/American Express/Visa, please give
number, expiry date and signature.*

_____

_____

*Name and address in block letters please:*

Name
_____

Address
_____

_____

_____